"I gave birth to our son seven months ago."

Dex didn't move. He didn't even breathe. "I have a son." It wasn't a question, but a statement of fact.

"Yes," Alyson said finally.

"Why didn't you tell me?" he demanded.

"I couldn't take the chance. I was afraid you'd try to take him away from me."

His face flushed with anger. "You should have trusted me to do the right thing. You should have damn well told me."

She let his anger buffet her. He was right. She'd known it in her heart all along. She should have told him. Despite her fear. Despite the risk. "I'm here now. I'm telling you now."

"*Why* are you here now, Alyson? Why did you pick *tonight* of all nights to tell me I had a son?"

"Because..." She forced her words through the thickness in her throat, through the fear tightening her lips. "Because he's gone."

Dear Harlequin Intrigue Reader,

Out like a lion! That's our Harlequin Intrigue lineup for March. As if you'd expect anything else.

Debra Webb concludes her trilogy THE SPECIALISTS with *Guardian of the Night*. Talk about sensuous and surreal and sexy. Man alive! You're sure to love this potent story that spans the night…and—to be sure—a lifetime. And you can find more COLBY AGENCY stories to follow this terrific spin-off later in the year.

Veteran Harlequin Intrigue author Patricia Rosemoor has created a new miniseries for you called CLUB UNDERCOVER. It's slick and secretive—just the way we like things here. *Fake I.D. Wife* is available this month and *VIP Protector* next month. So get your dancing shoes retreaded for this dynamic duo.

Finally we have two terrific theme promotions for you. *Claiming His Family* by Ann Voss Peterson is the newest addition to TOP SECRET BABIES. And *Marching Orders* by Delores Fossen kicks off MEN ON A MISSION. Who could ever resist a man in uniform?

So we hope you like our selections this month and we look forward to seeing you choose Harlequin Intrigue again for more great books of breathtaking romantic suspense.

Sincerely,

Denise O'Sullivan
Senior Editor
Harlequin Intrigue

CLAIMING
HIS FAMILY

ANN VOSS PETERSON

HARLEQUIN®

TORONTO • NEW YORK • LONDON
AMSTERDAM • PARIS • SYDNEY • HAMBURG
STOCKHOLM • ATHENS • TOKYO • MILAN • MADRID
PRAGUE • WARSAW • BUDAPEST • AUCKLAND

ISBN 0-373-22702-7

CLAIMING HIS FAMILY

ABOUT THE AUTHOR

Ever since she was a little girl making her own books out of construction paper, Ann Voss Peterson wanted to write. So when it came time to choose a major at the University of Wisconsin, creative writing was her only choice. Of course, writing wasn't a *practical* choice—one needs to earn a living. So Ann found jobs ranging from proofreading legal transcripts to working with quarter horses to washing windows. But no matter how she earned her paycheck, she continued to write the type of stories that captured her heart and imagination—romantic suspense. Ann lives near Madison, Wisconsin, with her husband, her two young sons, her Border collie and her quarter horse mare. Ann loves to hear from readers. E-mail her at ann@annvosspeterson.com or visit her Web site at annvosspeterson.com

Books by Ann Voss Peterson

HARLEQUIN INTRIGUE
579—INADMISSIBLE PASSION
618—HIS WITNESS, HER CHILD
647—ACCESSORY TO MARRIAGE
674—LAYING DOWN THE LAW
684—GYPSY MAGIC
        "Sabina"
702—CLAIMING HIS FAMILY

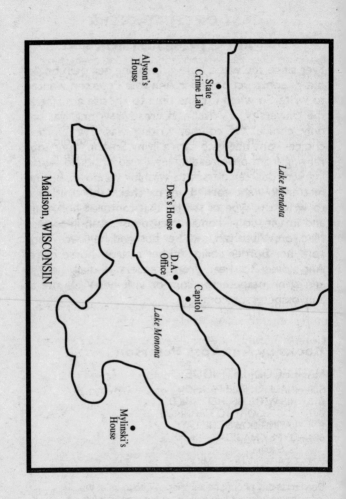

Madison, WISCONSIN

Alyson's
House

State
Crime Lab

Lake Mendota

Dex's House

D.A.
Office

Capitol

Lake Monona

Mylinski's
House

CAST OF CHARACTERS

Dex Harrington—A target of revenge, District Attorney Dex Harrington stands to lose everything he cares about: his career, his reputation and the child he never knew he had.

Alyson Fitzroy—A DNA analyst in Wisconsin's State Crime Lab, Alyson fell in love with Dex years ago. And when their relationship crumbled, so did her heart. But now she must go to him for help if she ever hopes to see their child again.

Andrew Clarke Smythe—The rapist is clever enough to get himself pardoned for his crimes. But that isn't enough. Now he wants revenge against the district attorney who put him in prison. And he'll do anything to get it.

John Cohen—Is the assistant district attorney cynical enough that he would sell out his office for cash?

Lee Runyon—How far will the top criminal defense attorney go to serve his clients?

Connie Rasula—Did she lie in order to get Smythe out of prison?

Maggie Daugherty—An employee of the D.A.'s office, Maggie holds a grudge against Alyson. But what is the real reason behind her narrowed eyes and severe frown?

Valerie D'Fonse—The brilliant scientist loves to gossip. But is there something sinister behind her wide smile?

Jennifer Scott—Is the crime lab chemist romantically involved with Andrew Smythe? Or is she part of the conspiracy to get him released?

Al Mylinski—He'll give his all to serve justice.

To Brett, a true labor of love.

Special thanks to Jerome Geurts, Director of Wisconsin
State Crime Lab—Madison for his help. Any errors,
omissions or creative license are mine alone.

Chapter One

Alyson Fitzroy stared at the television screen and ground her teeth together until the pain shooting along her jaw made her let up. A scene taped earlier in the day flickered on the ten o'clock news. Grinning broadly, Andrew Clarke Smythe swaggered to a waiting limousine, a small crowd of supporters cheering him on from outside the prison gates.

Andrew Clarke Smythe, the most notorious serial rapist in Dane County's history, was free. And the tests Alyson had performed in Wisconsin's State Crime Lab were responsible.

Since the day she'd received the order to perform the DNA comparison between blood found under the fingernails of a recent rape victim and the DNA of the imprisoned Smythe, she'd feared this would be the result. But she'd hoped the police would be able to shoot holes in the impossible theory that Smythe had a DNA clone out there committing rape—before he won his appeal for a new trial.

She'd never dreamed the governor would bypass the criminal justice system completely and give the Smythe Pharmaceuticals heir a pardon.

She wrapped her arms around herself. She felt sick to her stomach. But as sick as she felt, she knew it had to be worse for Dex.

As if echoing her thoughts, Dane County's new District Attorney Dex Harrington's face flashed on the television screen next. Outwardly he looked the same—the all-American male with hair the color of a sun-kissed beach and the square jaw and cleft chin of a superhero. But he'd changed in the past year and a half. She could read it in the hardness in his eyes, the rigid muscles along his jaw. He seemed even more judgmental than he had the last time she'd seen him. The time *she'd* been the one on whom he was passing judgment. The time she'd come up wanting.

She shoved the bitter memories from her mind. She couldn't waste her life being bitter. It wouldn't change anything. And looking at Dex's face on TV, the solemn line of his lips, the tortured squint of his eyes as he answered the reporters' questions, bitterness was far from her reach. She felt only regret.

Alyson pushed herself up from the couch and switched off the television. Wrapping her terry-cloth robe tighter around her, she padded out of her comfortable little living room on bare feet and started up the staircase leading to the bedrooms.

Reaching the top of the stairs, she strode past her own bedroom to the closed door at the end of the hall. She paused for a moment and listened. Hearing nothing, she turned the knob and pushed the door open.

Though Alyson had closed the windows against the humidity, the air still smelled like the fresh June night outside. She squinted her eyes against the darkness, the full moon obscured by drawn curtains. Only a feeble light from the hall chased away the shadows and revealed the white bars of the crib in the corner. The crib that held the most precious thing in her life.

She approached on stealthy steps and peered inside. Seven-month-old Patrick lay on his back, his head turned to the side. His little chest rose and fell with each breath. As always, a wave of love and gratitude surged through her at the sight of him. His peaceful face, his clenched fists, the tiny cleft in his chin.

Just like his daddy's.

She'd meant to tell Dex at first. Even after the blowup. After all, he'd had a right to know. She'd even telephoned him a few times, but he'd refused to take her calls. And whenever she'd forced herself to drive to his house, she'd invariably driven away without stepping from her car. She just couldn't make herself face him.

She'd kept seeing the scorn in his eyes when

she'd defended her father, when she'd taken her first wrong step. She'd kept hearing Dex's bitter words the last night they were together, the night he refused her a second chance, the night he told her he didn't want her anymore.

She shook her head, shutting out his words, and focused on her child's innocent face. No matter what Dex had done to her, he still deserved to know he had a child. And if things were that simple, she would have found a way to tell him.

But things weren't that simple.

Leaning over the crib gate, she reached a finger to touch the soft blond down on her baby's head. He'd given her the strength to go on after Dex's rejection, after her father's crimes and his subsequent death from his co-conspirator's bullet. Patrick was her little man, her love, her life. He was everything she had.

She couldn't risk losing him.

A feeling crept over her skin. A feeling that had nothing to do with the child sleeping in the crib. A feeling of being watched by malevolent eyes.

She jolted upright. Too late. A hand closed around her throat. A sweet-smelling cloth pressed over her nose and mouth.

She held her breath. She couldn't scream. If she did, she'd drag the fumes into her lungs, she'd lose consciousness. She wouldn't be able to fight. She kicked back, connecting with a shin.

A guttural growl exploded in the darkness. ''Damn bitch.''

She flailed her arms, trying to hit her attacker, trying to loosen his grip. Swinging low with one hand, she hit his hip, her fingers grasping something soft hanging from his belt. A rope. Oh, God, he intended to tie her up. Or just slip the ligature around her throat. Once that happened, she didn't stand a chance. Panic bolted through her. She flailed harder. One fist connected with the side of his face.

Another curse erupted from his lips. The hand on her throat tightened, cutting off her breath. Cutting off her life.

She hit him again, trying to put more force into the punch, but he only gripped her throat harder. Her pulse beat in her ears. Dizziness swam in her mind. Her fist connected again. She needed air. She couldn't let herself pass out.

Suddenly the grip on her throat loosened.

She gasped in a breath. Then another. She tried to twist in his grip, tried to get away, but he held her fast, the cloth clamped over her mouth and nose. The scent of chloroform tickled her sinuses and filled her lungs. Her head reeled, dizzy, slipping.

Darkness closed over her.

Chapter Two

Alyson woke, a strange smell filling her nostrils, its sweet flavor tainting her mouth. Her stomach protested and her head whirled. What had happened? She lay still, willing her stomach to stop flipping, her head resting on the berber carpet in Patrick's room.

Patrick.

Memories rushed back. The hand gripping her throat. The cloth over her mouth and nose. The unmistakable smell of chloroform.

She jolted into a sitting position. Her stomach heaved. Her head pounded. She choked back her sickness and climbed to her feet. Two steps and she was at the crib gate, her fingers clutching the bars, her mind scrambling to process what she was seeing—and what she was *not* seeing.

The crib sheet glowed like pristine snow. Shadows from the mobile suspended above the crib danced across the expanse of the sheet.

The *empty* expanse.

Patrick was gone.

Her heart lurched in her chest. She grabbed the side of the crib to keep from toppling over. It couldn't be. Her little man. Her baby.

She knelt beside the crib and looked underneath, straining her eyes, desperately searching the shadows. As if she believed he'd crawled out. As if she believed her seven-month-old was suddenly able to play a game of hide-and-seek with his mommy. Even in her panic, she knew he was gone. She knew it. But she didn't want to believe it. There had to be another explanation. There had to be, however impossible.

A phone's ring jangled above the roaring in her ears. Cold dread welled up inside her, swamping her, drowning her. She forced herself to concentrate. Forced herself to turn away from the empty crib. Forced herself to walk down the hall to her bedroom.

The telephone waited on a bedside table, its light throbbing in the shadows with each ring. She picked up the receiver and held it to her ear in a shaking hand. Far away she heard her voice say, "Hello?"

"I came for *you* tonight, Alyson." The voice slithered from the phone.

She gripped the receiver until her knuckles ached. "Where's my baby?"

"Like I said, I came for you tonight, but I found something better."

"Where's my baby?" Her voice broke, shrill with panic.

"He's safe. For now. But if you call the police, he won't be safe for long."

Oh, God. Oh, God. Her mind raced. She didn't know what to do. "Don't hurt him. Please. I'll pay you anything you want."

"I don't need your money."

"Then what? What do you want me to do?"

A chuckle erupted over the phone. "I was waiting for you to ask that. I want you to contact the baby's father."

"The baby's father?"

"You know who he is, don't you, Alyson? Or do you need to do a DNA test to find out?"

She did her best to swallow her panic. She had to stay calm. She had to stay focused. She had to convince this man she would do whatever he wanted. As long as he didn't hurt Patrick, as long as he gave her baby back, everything would be all right. "I know who he is."

"Good. It's much better when you don't have to rely on DNA. It's such an unpredictable science. All those double helixes running around, or whatever the hell. You never quite know when you're going to get an inconvenient match that will ruin all your plans."

Understanding cut through the fog of panic and confusion clouding her mind. The chloroform. The rope. All elements of the rapes he'd been convicted for two years ago. She knew who was on the other end. She knew who had stolen her baby. "Smythe."

"Can't put anything past you smart scientist types." A chuckle rippled over the phone line, vulgar, obscene. "How about that justice system? Isn't it great?"

"Why are you doing this?"

"Revenge. Pure and sweet." His voice lost the chuckle and grew dark. "You see, I know who fathered your bastard, too, Alyson. And no man condemns me to two years in that hellhole of a prison and gets away with it. No man. I want you to tell him that."

How in the world had Smythe learned Dex was Patrick's father? Alyson hadn't told a soul. She'd taken a leave of absence from work to hide her pregnancy. She hadn't even listed Dex on Patrick's birth certificate. But it didn't matter how Smythe had learned the truth, he was planning to use the baby against Dex. She couldn't let that happen. "Your plan isn't going to work, Smythe. Dex doesn't even know about Patrick."

"He will after you tell him."

Tell Dex? She couldn't tell Dex. Not now. Not after all this time. "But I—"

"You what?"

Her knees wobbled. She sank onto the bed, grasping the edge with one hand to keep her balance. "I'll do whatever you want. I'll tell him tonight."

"I thought you'd see things my way. You want me happy, Alyson. For your baby's sake, you want me happy. Understand?"

"Yes, I understand." She forced herself to breathe. She had to do something. Anything. Spotting the Memo button on the answering machine, she pushed it. At least she could get Smythe's voice on tape. She'd have proof of his threats. "After I tell Dex, then what?"

"I'll call."

"Can't you tell me more now? Can't I do something? Please." She couldn't just sit and wait. Not while Patrick was in the hands of this monster. Not while her baby was hungry and cold and wanted his mother. Not while Smythe might—

She bit the inside of her cheek until the coppery taste of blood tinged her mouth. She couldn't think about what Smythe might do to Patrick. She couldn't function if she thought about that.

"You just let Harrington know he has a son. I'll be in touch."

"Please. You can't do this. Give him back to—"

The line went dead.

ANDY SMYTHE pulled his sweet, red Corvette to the curb in front of the little ranch house and killed the engine. Alyson Fitzroy's questions and challenges still rang in his ears. Damn. A woman's mouth was only good for one thing, and it sure as hell wasn't talking. He couldn't stand women who talked too much. Especially the smart, superior types like Alyson Fitzroy. He would have loved to do what he'd gone to her house to do. He would have loved to grab her by her long red hair and put her in her place. He had been looking forward to it.

But then he'd seen the baby.

He glanced at the sleeping bundle next to him on the passenger seat. His little pajama-clad body. His nearly white hair that barely covered his scalp.

Andy had learned a lot about Dex Harrington while he'd been stewing in that hellhole. A lot about him. He knew Harrington and the redhead had been tight. They'd almost been married, the private investigator he'd hired had said. That's why Andy had chosen her as his first after getting out of prison. That coupled with the fact that she'd performed the DNA test that had gotten him out of prison seemed too ironic a combination to pass up. But seeing the kid had thrown him. He'd figured the kid had to be Harrington's.

Just as his chat with the redhead had confirmed.

Andy gathered the sleeping kid in his arms. Throwing the strap of the bag filled with baby things he'd swiped from the bedroom over his other shoul-

der, Andy climbed out of his Vette. He carried the
child to the door of the house and rang the bell.

A light blinked on in the bedroom. Great. Nanny
had been asleep. She wouldn't be happy with him
for waking her, but it couldn't be helped. As soon
as she saw the baby, she'd forgive him. Nanny never
could hold a grudge.

The frilly white curtain over the front door's small
window lifted and a withered eye peered out. It widened in surprise. The curtain fell and the door rattled
then opened.

"Do you know what time it is, Andy?" Nanny
stood in the doorway watching him with stern yet
gentle eyes, the way she used to every day when he
was growing up.

For a moment he felt like a puny little kid again,
crawling to Nanny for comfort after his mother had
treated him to another of her cruel and belittling
tirades.

He shoved the feeling aside and stepped past the
old woman and into the house. He would never be
puny and weak. Never again. And neither Dex Harrington's scathing words nor Alyson Fitzroy's superior tone would make it so. Tonight he hadn't
come for Nanny's comfort. He'd come for her help.
He walked into a tiny living room jammed with so
much furniture it would have looked like a ware-
house if not for the crocheted doilies covering every
surface.

Nanny followed him on tottering legs. "What do you have there? A child?"

He turned his best pitiful expression on her. "My child, Nanny. His mother doesn't want him. She abandoned him as soon as I was freed from prison."

"Your child? That child is too young. You were in prison when it was conceived."

"Haven't you heard of conjugal visits? They arrange them for prisoners, you know."

She nodded as if this was a totally plausible explanation.

Andy laughed to himself. If she bought that story, this was going to be easier than he'd thought. "I was in love with his mother. I wanted to marry her." He dropped his head as if he were ashamed. "Unfortunately she didn't feel the same way."

Pity and concern washed over Nanny's wrinkled face.

"I need your help, Nanny. I need you to take little Bart."

She frowned.

"You know me," he continued, "I can't take care of myself, let alone a baby."

"Well that's true enough."

"Besides, I want my son to have the best care a boy can have. I want him to have the only thing that was good about my childhood. I want him to have you."

Nanny's old face softened into a smile. Amazing.

Sometimes he didn't even have to come up with a lie to manipulate people. Sometimes he had only to tell the truth.

She held out her arms for the baby. "Give him here. I hate to see you worrying about your poor child, Andy. Not after all you've been through. You're right. He's better off with me."

Andy placed the baby in her arms and set the bag on the floor. Then he slipped his wallet from his pocket and pulled out a wad of hundreds and set them on a crocheted doily.

The old lady eyed him, hardness stealing back into her face. "I'm not taking your money, boy."

"The baby needs things. I want my son to have the best. This money is for him."

She paused then nodded, her thin, wrinkled lips stretching into a smile once again. "You're a good daddy, Andy, taking care of your baby this way. I'm proud of you."

Andy couldn't keep the grin off his face. A good daddy. That was him. A regular chip off the old Smythe block. He stifled his laugh until he bade the old woman goodbye and closed the door behind him.

The baby would be safe and well cared for with Nanny. Contrary to what he'd told the redhead, he had no intention of hurting the kid. He wasn't a sicko, unlike some of the scumbags he'd done time with. And he was no baby killer, either. The baby was safe.

But the father? Not a chance. The baby would give Andy just the leverage he needed to turn Dex Harrington's life into a living nightmare. And in the process, he'd see he got a piece of the oh-so-superior redhead, too.

Revenge would be sweet.

ALYSON GRIPPED the wheel with white-knuckled fingers and struggled to quell the trembling that claimed every nerve. Stomping on the accelerator as hard as she dared, she steered her Volvo around sharp corners and down quiet streets. She trained her eyes on the road ahead, keeping her gaze from wandering to the rearview mirror, to the reflection of the empty child's safety seat belted in back.

She couldn't give in to the panic, the rush of loss that threatened to overwhelm her. She had to stay rational. She had to reach Dex. She had to get Patrick back.

And whatever that took, she'd do it.

The roofline of Dex's sprawling old bungalow loomed on the edge of the lake, a dark shadow against the moonlight-kissed waves beyond. Alyson swerved onto the dead end street, pulled to the curb and scrambled from the car.

Built into the bank of Lake Mendota, Dex's house was his pride and joy. Alyson could still picture the satisfaction on his face the day he'd bought the scarred old former fraternity house and started putting his renovation plans into motion. It was as if he'd finally arrived, finally proven he had transcended his desolate upbringing.

Her heart pounded in her ears, drowning out the lapping of the waves against the shore. The humid June air clogged her throat. She climbed the stone steps and stepped onto the porch. A light shone from the back of the house. Pressing a trembling finger to the doorbell, she held her breath.

A chime sounded through the old structure. Footsteps thudded on the hardwood floor inside. The door opened.

"Alyson." Dex stood silhouetted against light glowing behind him. But even in the shadow she could see his brow furrow, the muscles along his cleft chin hardening in unswerving judgment.

Some things never changed. But his judgment of her didn't matter. Not anymore. The only thing that mattered now was Patrick. Alyson forced her voice to function. "I need to talk to you."

Behind his wire-rimmed glasses, his midnight-blue eyes seemed to grow darker, harder. He took in a deep breath and expelled it. "I suppose you heard about the governor's pardon."

"Yes."

"Is that what you need to talk about?"

"In part, yes."

"Is it something about the testing you did? Something I should know?"

After Smythe's pardon today it was logical Dex would assume she was coming to see him about the DNA test she'd done—the test that had sprung the rapist from prison. "No. It's not that. The testing was accurate. The two samples were a match."

His gaze raked over her, as if trying to determine her true motive for showing up on his doorstep.

"I need your help." Her words trembled with barely controlled panic. "It's urgent."

As if hearing the edge in her voice, he gave a succinct nod and backed from the doorway, allowing her inside.

As she stepped into the house, a shiver stole up her spine. Sights, smells and feelings from the past washed over her. The tickle of dust in her nose as she and Dex hauled box after box of ancient junk from the attic after he bought the house. The scent of paint, varnish and wallpaper paste as they reclaimed the scarred walls and floors. The sound of hers and Dex's laughter mingling and filling the empty halls. Memories of happy times, before her father's crimes, before she learned exactly how precarious her position was in Dex's heart.

She shut the memories out of her mind. They were merely sentimental longing. And she didn't have time for sentiment. "Can we sit down?"

His eyes narrowed to suspicious slits. "You can't tell me here?"

Her knees quivered. "Please. I need to sit down. And so should you."

He raised his brows at her last comment. But instead of grilling her further, he mercifully turned and led her through the house.

She followed, forcing her eyes to move over her surroundings. Forcing her mind to focus on something safer than the panic thrashing inside her, threatening to shred what little control she had.

Dex had changed things since she'd helped him decorate following the renovation. He'd replaced the simple curtains she'd chosen with wood-slat blinds. He'd furnished the rooms with heavy leather instead of the light-fabric couches and chairs she'd helped him select. It was as if he'd obliterated her from his life. As if she'd ceased to exist in his world.

And of course, she had.

But he'd never disappeared from her world. His presence went far deeper than blinds and furniture. She felt his presence every time she looked into Patrick's blue eyes or kissed that tiny cleft chin.

Patrick.

Panic rose in her throat like bile. Choking it back, she followed Dex into the glassed-in porch they used to sit in together watching thunderstorms come in off the lake. He gestured to a wicker chair. She took her place among the cushions.

He lowered himself into a chair facing her. "We're sitting. What is it?"

She tangled her fingers together in her lap and took a deep breath. There were so many things that had been said between them. And even more things that had not been said. Before she told him about Patrick, she had to give him some idea why she hadn't told him about his son. She had to make him understand. "I tried calling you. Several times. After my father was killed. You refused my calls. And you didn't call back when I left messages on your machine."

Dex's brows snapped low over his eyes. "I didn't want to talk to you, Alyson. I don't want to rehash the past. I hope that's not why you came here tonight."

"You turned your back on me, Dex. And my only crime was that I loved my father."

He stood and paced the length of the sunporch. He stopped, his back to her, his shoulders obviously tight under his crisp white dress shirt. Slowly he turned to look at her with hard eyes. "Your father was a criminal. The worst kind of criminal. He used his title of district attorney to sell justice. He perverted the entire system. And you defended him."

"He was my *father*. I didn't believe he could do something like that."

"You didn't want to believe it. You didn't want to believe *me*."

She swallowed into a dry throat. "That's why I called. That's what I wanted to tell you. I was wrong about my father. That I was sorry I didn't believe you when you first told me what you suspected. But that's not the only thing I wanted to tell you."

"What are you saying? Why are you here, Alyson?"

"I wanted to tell you I was pregnant." She rubbed clammy hands over her jeans and willed herself to look at Dex, to meet his gaze. "I gave birth to our son seven months ago."

Dex didn't move. He didn't even seem to breathe. "I have a son." It wasn't a question, but a statement of fact.

"Yes."

He folded himself into a chair. Taking off his glasses, he rubbed a hand over his face. "Why didn't you tell me?"

"You wouldn't take my calls, remember?"

"You could have come to see me. You could have made me listen."

She could have. She'd known it then, and she knew it now. If she'd really wanted to tell Dex, she wouldn't have let anything stop her. "I was afraid."

"Afraid of what?"

"Afraid you would take him away from me."

A muscle tensed along his jawline. "Why the hell would you think that?"

She shot him an incredulous look. What she'd

done had been wrong, cowardly. But she'd had reason. "Because you hated me, Dex. You were so hard and uncaring and judgmental. You shut me out of your life and wouldn't give me a second chance. And after what my father did, there isn't a judge in Dane County who wouldn't be biased against me in a custody fight, wrong or not."

"So you thought I would use your father's sins to convince the court you were an unfit mother?"

"I couldn't take the chance."

His face flushed with anger. Cords of muscle stood out along his neck. "First you believed I was lying about your father, then you believed I would rob my son of a mother. What kind of a rotten SOB do you think I am?"

"I don't— I didn't— I was afraid."

"You should have trusted me to do the right thing. You should have damn well told me."

She sat still and let his anger buffet her. He was right, she'd known it in her heart all along. She should have told him. Despite her fear. Despite the risk. "I'm here now. I'm telling you now."

"*Why* are you here now, Alyson? Why did you pick *tonight* of all nights to tell me I have a son?"

"Because…" She forced the words through the thickness in her throat, through the fear tightening her lips. "Because he's gone."

Chapter Three

"Gone?" Dex's heart stuttered in his chest. He shot up from his chair, muscles tensed to fight. "What the hell do you mean?"

Alyson took in a shaky breath as if trying to hold back tears. "I went into Patrick's room to check on him, and Smythe grabbed me. He pressed a chloroform-soaked cloth over my face. When I woke up, Patrick was gone. Smythe took him."

"Smythe? Are you sure?" Dex had been living and breathing Andrew Clarke Smythe in the months since the DNA match had been made. But to now learn he had a son, and that Andrew Clarke Smythe had kidnapped him, was too surreal to absorb.

"Smythe called me. Somehow he knew you were Patrick's father. He took our baby to get back at you for convicting him two years ago."

Rage, pure and hot, surged through Dex's blood. Smythe had kidnapped his son. *His son.* If the son of a bitch wanted to make things personal, he'd succeeded. And he'd soon wish he hadn't. If Dex had anything to say about it, the scum would be strung up before daybreak. Crossing to the door in three strides, he left Alyson huddled on the porch. His footsteps thundered down the hall, echoing on the hardwood floor like the beat of war drums. Reaching the library, he circled his desk and reached for the cordless phone perched on the credenza.

"Wait."

Finger poised over the number pad, he looked up into Alyson's emerald eyes.

"Smythe told me if we got the police involved, I would never see Patrick again." Her voice broke. Her eyes filled with tears, but she didn't let them wind down her cheeks. "If you call the police, he'll find out. He said he has sources. He could have someone watching us right now."

She was probably right about Smythe's sources. Heir to Smythe Pharmaceuticals, the poor little rich boy had endless money at his disposal. And money could corrupt even the purest police department. Or district attorney's office. Dex had seen it happen.

Expelling a long breath, he set the cordless phone on the desk and studied her face in the library's bright light. Fine lines framed her mouth and eyes. Shadows lurked in the hollows under her cheek-bones, making her normally smooth face appear almost gaunt. He'd seen these signs of stress many times in his work. Hell, he'd grown up surrounded by desperation. "So what else did Smythe say?"

"I have a tape. I recorded part of what he said." She pulled a tiny cassette from her pocket and held it out to Dex with shaking fingers.

Dex took the tape from her hand. After rummaging through his desk, he produced a microcassette recorder and slipped the tape inside. He pushed the play button.

Andrew Smythe's voice wound through the library, smooth as a snake's hiss. Dex had heard it many times in press conferences after court, in pleas from prison, and it always sounded the same. No fear. No pity. Nothing but an unfeeling smugness that set Dex's teeth on edge.

Much more striking was the sound of Alyson's voice. So naked. So desperate.

Dex tried to steel himself against the vulnerability in her voice. He tried to focus on Smythe's words. On what he was saying. Only when the tape ended did he allow himself to look at her.

Her eyes searched his, desperate for answers. Answers he couldn't give.

He ejected the cassette. "That's Smythe, all right. But there are no threats on the tape. Nothing I can use to convince a judge to grant an arrest warrant."

Her gaze fell to the desktop. "I must not have pressed the button soon enough."

"What did Smythe say? Exactly. Think."

"He said I should tell you that Patrick is your son."

He gritted his teeth. If Smythe hadn't demanded she tell him about Patrick, he never would have known. That was clear enough. And that knowledge stabbed into him with the force of a sharp blade in malevolent hands.

He clamped down on the bleeding. What Alyson would or wouldn't have done wasn't important anymore. "What else did he say?"

"That he'd be in touch with us. And he'd let us know what to do next."

Dex grimaced. That's what he was afraid of. Leveling her with hard eyes, he shook his head. "I'm not playing a part in any twisted puppet show Smythe has planned."

Her eyes widened. Leaning toward him, she gripped the edge of the desk. "If we do what he says, he'll give Patrick back."

"Smythe has no intention of returning Patrick."

"But he said—"

"I don't care what he said. He's not going to give Patrick back to us, even if we play by every one of his damn rules. Smythe wants to humiliate me, to dominate me, to win. That's what he's about. Not fairness. Not keeping his word."

"He'll—" She swayed, clutching the desk for balance.

Dex circled the desk. He slipped his arm around her shoulders and propped her up.

After guiding her a few steps, he lowered her into a chair. The soft scents of chamomile and roses surrounded him, a bittersweet memory. Love. Trust. Things he'd once hoped they had together. Things they'd never really had at all. Finally he straightened, spun away from her and paced across the floor.

She gripped the chair's leather arms and held on. "We can't take the chance, Dex. We have to do what he says. I can't lose my baby."

"We aren't going to lose him." Though his voice barely rose above a whisper, it rang with the determination he felt deep in his gut. "I know Smythe. And what I don't know, I'm damn well going to find out. I'll get our son back. If you want to help, you'll have to trust me for once in your life."

Alyson raised her chin. Tears glittered in her eyes, making them sparkle like emeralds. Her lips tightened. "Why? What do you want me to do?"

Just as he'd thought. She didn't trust him any more now than she had the day he'd told her that her father was selling plea bargains. An ache crept up his spine and settled in his shoulders. More than a year had passed since he'd last seen Alyson. His feelings of bitterness and betrayal should be dead and buried by now. But they'd returned the moment he'd opened the door tonight and seen her distraught face. Smelling her scent and hearing the vulnerability in her voice had only deepened the ache.

And now to learn he had a son. They had a son. Together...

Pressure constricted his chest, tighter than a steel band. He shoved the thoughts and feelings aside. He couldn't let himself think about what having a son might mean. He had to focus. He had to formulate some kind of plan. And the first part of that plan was to ensure Smythe didn't have the opportunity to strike again. "I want you to go home. Try to get some sleep. I'll arrange for plain clothes officers to watch your house. Smythe and his sources will never know they're cops."

Her eyes grew wide with alarm. "You can't shut me out. I need to help find Patrick."

"I'm not shutting you out. I'll call as soon as I learn anything."

She raised her chin in that determined way of hers and shook her head. "I'm not going anywhere."

"You need to be home in case Smythe calls."

"I forwarded the calls to my cell phone. If he calls, I can answer wherever I am." She dipped a hand into her pocket and pulled out a phone as an offer of proof. "I know you don't want to have anything to do with me, Dex. For God's sake, you didn't before you knew I didn't tell you about Patrick. But I can't just sit at home knowing that monster has him. Surely you can understand that."

He could understand far too much about how Alyson must be feeling, even after all this time. That was the problem. And it would be even more of a problem if Smythe had figured that out. And from all indications, he had. "If you stay home, I can arrange for protection. The police can turn your house into a regular fortress. If you don't, you'll make things much tougher."

"Protection? For me?"

"Yes, for you. You said Smythe used chloroform on you when he broke into your house tonight."

"Yes."

"I'm betting he was also carrying rope."

He could tell by her expression the answer was yes. She shook her head hard, her auburn hair lashing her cheeks. Obviously she'd guessed where he was going. And she didn't want to hear it.

Tough. She had to face facts. He had. "Smythe isn't a kidnapper, Alyson. He isn't a man who targets children, either. He rapes women. He was planning to get his revenge on me by attacking you."

Though she seemed to know what was coming, a shudder still shook her.

He fought the need to rush to her side again, to encircle her with his arm and let her lean against him. "Are you okay?"

Gripping the chair until her knuckles turned white, she nodded. "So you think he came after me and stumbled on Patrick."

"That's what I'm guessing. He must have figured out Patrick was my child, and that kidnapping him would present an even greater opportunity for revenge."

"But if that's true, why didn't he rape me, too?"

"Do you remember what he did to those other women?"

She pulled back in her chair as if flinching from her own thoughts. "He kidnapped them."

Dex nodded. "He took them to a private place— a place no one would discover them—and he raped them for hours. His last victim was attacked for days. I'm sure he wanted to do the same to you, but he couldn't handle kidnapping both you and Patrick at the same time."

"So he settled for Patrick."

"For now." Dex looked her straight in the eye. He hated being this blunt, but Alyson had to face the facts. Smythe had Patrick, and she was next. And who knew what other targets Smythe had on his list? No one or nothing Dex had ever cared about was safe.

"But how did he know about us, Dex? We didn't exactly announce our relationship from the rooftops. How would he know that you and I were once involved? That Patrick was your child?"

"That's one of the things I'm going to find out."

Straightening her spine, she set her chin. "So where do we start?"

"We keep you safe. I'll post officers outside your house twenty-four seven. And I'll look into getting you an alarm system. I'll keep you updated on everything I learn. I promise."

"No. I'm not going to stay trapped in my house. I don't care what Smythe is planning. I have to do something to get my baby back." Tears spiked her lashes, but her voice carried a note of determination.

"Alyson—"

"I mean it, Dex. If you don't let me help you, I'll figure something out on my own."

The thought of Alyson by his side made his shoulders ache like a son of a bitch. But he couldn't let her walk around without protection.

Thrusting himself to his feet, Dex paced across the room. Damn Smythe and his sick revenge. Damn the governor and his pardons. And damn Alyson for failing to tell him he had a son until the baby was kidnapped.

But most of all, damn *him* for letting her latest betrayal wound him all over again.

He strode for the door without looking at her. He couldn't. Looking at her would only make him want to take her into his arms again when he would be far better off to run in the other direction. "There are fresh sheets in the guest room closet. We'll leave for the prison where Smythe was incarcerated first thing in the morning."

LOCATED IN GRANT COUNTY, a skip and a jump from the Mississippi River, the Grant Correctional Institute loomed on one of the few plateaus in an area of sharp hills and sweeping gorges—Wisconsin's unglaciated region. Alyson had always thought the area was beautiful. But today she hardly noticed the scenery whizzing past the car window. She hardly noticed anything except the man sitting next to her, his hands gripping the steering wheel.

Tall and fit, he looked every bit as appealing as the first time she'd met him. The pull of attraction had reached into her chest and grabbed her by the heart when her father had introduced her to his protégé, the newest assistant district attorney in the office. But it wasn't until she'd talked to him later that night, until she'd seen his intelligence and humor and idealism that she'd lost her heart.

And she still hadn't recovered it. Of course now it was bloody and wounded. Damaged goods. As was she. Especially in Dex's eyes.

No matter what had happened between them, she could never regret their time together. She couldn't even regret her shattered heart. Because if it weren't for Dex, she wouldn't have Patrick. And any kind of pain was worth enduring for one moment of holding her little boy in her arms.

Patrick. Her arms ached to hold him. When she'd awakened this morning, she'd felt more alone than the day her father died. Even the months of hiding her pregnancy, going through childbirth and waking at night to care for Patrick hadn't been as hard. Now Patrick was gone. Now she had no one. And no way of ensuring that her baby was safe and fed and cared for.

She focused on the road ahead. "What are we looking for at the prison?"

"Someone helped Smythe smuggle his blood out. That's the only way it could have ended up under that woman's fingernails—the woman who claims she was raped."

"So we check the prison sign-in sheet?"

"And phone logs. I want to see who he's been talking to."

"I assume you've questioned the alleged rape victim?"

"The police talked to her when she reported the rape. But she disappeared right after your lab discovered the blood was a match with Smythe's. Area sheriffs' departments have been looking for her ever since. That leaves only the person who smuggled Smythe's blood out of prison."

"Maybe that person was her. What was her name?"

"Connie Rasula. And it's doubtful she did the smuggling. The police found nothing to tie her to Smythe. And they looked hard, believe me."

She could imagine. No one in law enforcement

liked to be thrown a curve ball like the one they'd been tossed. If they couldn't clear up the question about Smythe's DNA double, DNA evidence could be called into question in courtrooms across the country. But to her, that possibility paled in comparison to the prospect of never seeing her son again. "So we find out who visited him."

Dex nodded, his gaze glued to the twisting road ahead. "And hope we come away with some answers."

"Hope? That isn't very reassuring."

"It's all I have. If you have a better idea, spit it out."

Alyson bit her bottom lip and stared out the windshield as Dex pulled the car up to the outer gate of the prison. Rolls of razor wire glinted in the sun. Sharp and brutal and unforgiving.

She shivered. Just the thought of venturing inside the gates with the kind of men she did her part to put behind bars every day—men like Andrew Smythe—made her skin crawl. But if it meant finding a name on those visitor logs or phone records that would lead them to Patrick, she would walk a gauntlet through the cell blocks alone.

She glanced at Dex. Jaw set and eyes narrowed, he looked ready to fight the world. Despite his anger toward her, despite his judgment of her, despite all that had happened between them, he was with her now. And he would fight with her to find their son.

For the first time in over a year, she didn't have to fight alone.

DEX LEANED against the stainless-steel counter in the prison vestibule and paged through the visitor's log, scanning for Smythe's name in the Inmate Visited column. Alyson stood beside him, close enough to read the names scrawled on the battered pages. Too close. Her body heat made the already warm day that much warmer. Her sweet scent teased his senses. And when she moved her head, wisps of auburn hair trailed across his arm.

Having her sleep under his roof last night had been pure torture. Even though the master bedroom was on the main floor of his house and the guest bedroom was upstairs, she'd been far too close to afford him any semblance of a night's sleep. And even when he did manage to shut his eyes, dreams of the son he'd never seen haunted him.

He forced his attention to the names in the sign-in book. He had to concentrate. He had to find a lead, any lead, that would take him to Patrick. They'd found nothing of note in the prison's telephone logs. Only an occasional call to Smythe's lawyer. He prayed these pages would reveal something. Because they had nothing but Smythe's word that Patrick would be safe. And Dex knew just how little Andrew Clarke Smythe's word was worth.

Alyson grasped Dex's hand before he could turn

the next page, her fingers clamping around his. "There." She pointed to Smythe's name on the form. Tracing her finger along the page, she landed on the name of the visitor. She exhaled. "Oh. Lee Runyon again."

Dex nodded, noting several more entries for Runyon on the following pages. "He must have been working on an appeal." As Smythe's attorney, Runyon had flooded the appellate court with a constant stream of paperwork on Smythe's behalf. All the appeals money could buy. It was no wonder he had to telephone and visit his client often.

"That doesn't mean Runyon isn't helping Smythe in other ways. Making contacts for him. Helping with arrangements," Alyson said.

Dex had never liked Runyon much. No district attorney did. He won far too many cases he should lose. He had a way of charming the jury and creating a smoke screen around his client that blurred the truth. And he had an overactive ego. But that didn't mean he was a criminal. Or that he would cross that line, even for a client with as much money as Smythe. "I suppose it's possible."

"But not probable?"

"No. Not unless he has a damn good reason for risking everything he's built."

Alyson nodded, but the narrowed look of suspicion in her eyes didn't let up.

Dex skimmed over the remaining entries in the

visitor's log. He flipped page after page until there were no more pages to flip. Besides Runyon, no other name showed up as a visitor for Smythe.

"Wait." Alyson grabbed his hand again. "There's a page missing from the book."

Dex paged back. Sure enough. The page numbers skipped from twenty to twenty-two. He raised his eyes to the corrections officer behind the bulletproof glass. "There's a page missing from this visitor's log. Do you know anything about this?"

The stocky woman shook her head. "No, sir. But I'll check for it back here." She disappeared into the office where the visitor logs were archived.

"Wait a second. Maybe we can…" Alyson leaned over the book, straining for a closer look. A wisp of silky hair trailed across Dex's hand. Her breast pressed against his arm. Heat stirred inside him. Heat he didn't want to feel. He stepped back, allowing her free access to the log.

She examined the page, her freckled nose mere inches from the paper. Suddenly she shot up from the book and turned to him, her face animated, her eyes glowing like green embers. "There's an impression of the writing from the missing page on this page. Look." She moved to the side, allowing Dex to examine the paper.

Sure enough, inkless lines had been etched into the page by the force of the pen writing on the now missing page. Adrenaline spiked his blood. He opened his briefcase, located a pencil and tore a blank piece of paper from a legal pad. Placing the paper over the log page, he traced across it lightly with the pencil until the etched impressions came into focus.

Although the lines jumbled with other writing in the log, he could make out the name "Smythe" in the middle of the page. He kept tracing. Another name took form in the visitor column of the log. His jaw clenched.

"What?" Alyson looked from his face to the book. "What do you see?" She leaned close.

Dex gritted his teeth. "There might be a logical explanation. There had *better* be a logical explanation."

Alyson turned wide eyes on him once more. "For what? I can't make it out. Whose name do you see?"

Dex traced the name with his finger. "John Cohen."

Alyson's eyes widened.

Of course she would know the man. John Cohen had worked in the district attorney's office longer than Dex had. Nearly as long as her father, Neil Fitzroy. And John and Fitz had shared political affiliations.

Alyson swallowed hard and shifted her feet, soles scraping against waxed tile. "Why would John Cohen visit Smythe?"

Dex shoved memories of Neil Fitzroy's scheme to sell justice to the back of his mind. For now. Maybe John had a good reason for visiting Smythe. Maybe there was also a good reason for the page with his signature on it to go missing. Maybe. But the ache in Dex's shoulders said something different. "That's what I'm damn well going to find out."

Chapter Four

Alyson walked through the door Dex held open and into the jumble of aromas and laughter in the Schettler Brew Pub. Her stomach knotted with tension. She clutched her hands together in front of her to keep them from trembling.

She scanned the crowd of faces. A pair of dark eyes met hers. Eyes that belonged to the receptionist at the district attorney's office. Maggie Daugherty had joined the district attorney's office only a year before Alyson's father died, but she had always been so open and friendly, Alyson used to think of her as a sister. Or at least a friend. But judging by the way Maggie narrowed her eyes at the sight of Alyson and Dex together, Alyson's fears about venturing into the brew pub were more than justified. No doubt other D.A.'s office employees would lose their smiles when they spotted her. The pariah. Neil Fitzroy's daughter.

She shouldn't have come here. Shouldn't have

come to the spot Dex said had become the after-work hangout for A.D.A.s—assistant district attorneys. She should have done as Dex wanted and let him handle questioning John Cohen.

No.

She raised her chin and stepped forward into the pub. She would face whatever scorn she had to, to find Patrick. Even the contempt of the whole damn town. And if John Cohen was carrying on her father's legacy, if he had helped Smythe in exchange for money, she would face that, too.

Dex leading the way, she marched across the hardwood floor and wound through tables and patrons until they reached a vacant spot at the bar. Jovial laughter and conversation jangled in her ears. Laughter and conversation that stilled as she bellied up to the bar.

Trying to appear oblivious to the stares, she focused straight ahead. Two men worked behind the gleaming oak bar, tapping the famous Schettler beer and chatting with patrons. But one of the men wasn't a bartender by trade. Not by a long shot. The tall, dark-haired Texan serving drinks and hobnobbing with his fellow district attorneys after work was one of the best and most dedicated prosecutors in this or any other county. And he used to be her father's right-hand man.

The man her father had tried to kill.

"It's about time you joined us down here, Dex."

Dillon Reese's smoky drawl rose over the laughter and hum of voices in the bar. "You haven't been in here since my wedding."

Dex gave him a nod. "I don't want to do too much socializing with the troops, you know. Bad for the image. Pretty soon they'll start seeing me as human."

"No one would make that mistake." Dillon lowered one lid in a teasing wink.

Alyson was surprised by the camaraderie forged between the two men. They hadn't seen eye-to-eye on anything before her father's death. Of course, her father had nurtured the rift between them.

Dillon gave Dex one last grin before focusing on her. The smile fell from his lips. "Howdy, Alyson."

Somewhere she found the strength to nod. "Dillon."

A thousand beats of her heart passed before he spoke again. "The Hefe Weizen is wonderful. You should try it. Jacqueline really outdid herself on this one." His lips stretched into a gentle smile. An accepting smile. "On the house."

Alyson's breath escaped in a tortured whoosh. Dillon Reese had a heart the size of his native state if he could welcome her after what her father had tried to do to him and the woman he had since married. "Thanks, Dillon."

As if she'd heard Alyson's thoughts, Jacqueline Schettler Reese rounded the corner into the bar, flashing her husband a wide smile. Even though she was dressed in a boxy apron, the round shape of her pregnant tummy was clearly visible.

Neil Fitzroy's crimes against Jacqueline were the worst of all. He and his accomplice, Buck Swain, had tried to kill Jacqueline's daughter to keep her quiet after she'd witnessed her own father's murder. Alyson had never met Jacqueline. And even after Dillon's reaction, she didn't want to meet her now.

"Dillon, I have to go pick up Amanda from her gymnastics class. Can you hold down the fort until the night shift gets set up?"

"Sure thing, darlin'."

Jacqueline's gaze landed on Dex. She gave him a big smile and poked her husband in the shoulder. "Haven't you gotten Dex a beer yet, Dillon? It isn't often we have the district attorney himself here. How are you doing, Dex?"

Dex returned her smile. "Nice seeing you again, Jacqueline."

Jacqueline's gaze moved to Alyson. "Aren't you going to introduce us?"

Alyson held her breath. She would give anything to crawl into a hole about now.

Dex didn't even flinch. "This is Alyson Fitzroy."

Jacqueline's blue eyes widened. "Alyson—"

"Fitzroy." Alyson pulled herself up, ready to take Jacqueline's contempt square in the face. "I'm sorry for the hell my father put you through."

Jacqueline took a deep breath. When she exhaled, a polite smile lifted the corners of her lips. "Thank you. I'm sorry for the hell he put you through, as well."

Alyson's throat closed. Since her father's death she'd felt ostracized from her former life, her former friends. People who knew she was Neil Fitzroy's daughter had cooled toward her as if her father's sins had tainted her. She'd lost more than Dex and her father the day Neil Fitzroy died. She'd lost who she was—who she used to be.

Never had she expected to be welcomed by Dillon and Jacqueline. Never had she dreamed she'd be welcomed back into the fold by the two people her father had hurt most. "Thank you."

Dex looked down at her.

A chill sank into her bones.

Jacqueline's and Dillon's acceptance was small comfort when faced with the hard line of Dex's mouth and the judgmental glint in his eye. She'd lost so much. So much that she'd never get back. No matter how much kindness strangers showed her, she could never regain the relationship that had meant the most to her. She could never undo the choices she'd made.

"So what will it be? Dex? Alyson?" Dillon drawled. "Two pints of Hefe Weizen have your names on them."

Dex held up a hand. He really should take Dillon up on the offer sometime, try to do more to smooth over the rift that had been between them. But now wasn't the time. "We'll have to take a rain check, Dillon. I need to talk to Cohen. Thought he might be down here. Have you seen him?"

Dillon nodded and pointed to a booth in the corner. Tall and thin, John Cohen hunched over a beer alone. Perfect. He nodded his thanks to Dillon and started across the pub.

Alyson walked close enough behind for him to catch the ghost of her scent, even over the aromas of cigarette smoke, fried food and beer. He'd tried to talk her out of coming to the Schettler Brew Pub. As angry as he was with her, he didn't want to see her hurt. And he'd been sure coming here, digging into old wounds Fitz had left in his wake, would only hurt her.

He blew a relieved sigh through tense lips. Leave it to Dillon and Jacqueline to push aside their hatred for Fitz to embrace his daughter. Now if Dex could only push aside his concern for Alyson and focus on getting answers from Cohen, maybe they would get somewhere.

Reaching his destination, Dex folded himself into the booth, opposite Cohen. He moved over enough for Alyson to slide in next to him. "Hello, Cohen."

Cohen looked up from his beer. A smile touched with the fine edge of cynicism spread over his lips.

"Dex. Finally coming down from your ivory tower to join in the fun?"

Cynicism wasn't uncommon in the district attorney's office. God knew they dealt with enough nasty people doing nasty things to one another to get a bit jaded over the years. But John Cohen elevated cynicism to an art form. Dex gestured to the bar. "The fun looks like it's going on over there, Cohen. Not here."

"Are you saying I'm not fun?" Cohen shrugged. "What else is new?" Cohen's gaze flicked to Alyson. He sized her up with deep brown eyes that had no doubt melted a few women's hearts along the way. This time, the smile that spread over his lips was one of pure amusement. "I'll be damned. I haven't seen you in a long time, Alyson."

Alyson smiled and nodded. "We have some questions for you, John."

Cohen crooked a brow and glanced from Alyson to Dex. "So the two of you are a 'we' again?"

"No," Dex said without looking at Alyson. He couldn't bear to see the hurt look on her face. He leveled a pointed stare on Cohen. "We just came from the prison in Grantsville." Dex paused, watching Cohen's eyes.

If Cohen had any reaction, he hid it well.

Dex pushed on. "It seems you've been out there recently, as well."

"And you want to know why?" Cohen's gaze

darted away from them and landed on a waitress walking toward him with a plate stacked with a burger and thick wedges of fried potatoes. "About time. I'm famished."

The waitress served the food. "Would you like to order?"

"No. Thank you," Dex said without taking his eyes from Cohen.

Next to him, he could feel Alyson shake her head. Satisfied everyone was taken care of, the waitress left.

"So why were you at the prison, Cohen?"

Cohen paused, seemingly sorting through his memory. "What prison was that?"

Dex balled his hands into fists beneath the table. If the A.D.A. didn't start giving him some straight answers, he'd either have to charge him with conspiracy or beat him to a bloody pulp.

"The one near Grantsville. Grant County," Alyson supplied.

"Oh, yeah. I went there to talk to Smythe, your rapist the governor just let loose." He eyed Dex, one corner of his lips crooking into a cynical grin. "But of course, that's why you're asking, isn't it?"

"What did you talk to him about?"

Cohen took a bite of burger. "Damn. I forgot to ask for ketchup. I can't stand being without ketchup." He set the burger on his plate and opened the briefcase set beside him on the table. Reaching inside, he pulled out a handful of foil packets containing ketchup. Ripping open a packet, he spread the condiment on his burger. He ripped open another packet.

One more evasion and Dex would have to risk an assault charge. "Put down the damned ketchup, Cohen."

John Cohen raised surprised eyes to his face.

"What did you talk to Smythe about?"

Sighing, Cohen set down the ketchup and shook his head. "Nothing earth-shattering. Same old, same old. Remember that assault case where one convict jumped another in the county lockup? Just about killed the guy?"

"I remember."

"Smythe was a witness. It happened a while ago, back when he was still in jail, before he was transferred to Grantsville."

Dex leaned forward in the booth. "The page you signed in on in the visitor's log was missing. Do you know anything about that?"

Cohen bit into his burger. When he finished chewing, he shrugged. "What is all this about, Dex? You think I helped Smythe stage that recent rape? Shades of Fitz?"

Dex tried not to notice Alyson squirm beside him. She raised her chin in that damned determined way of hers. "Did you?"

Cohen turned his smile on her. "Although I can

almost understand Fitz using the system for his own profit, I do still have enough scruples left not to unleash a rapist scumbag like Smythe on the public. To answer your question, no, I didn't help Smythe.''

Dex narrowed his eyes. He wanted to believe Cohen. But then what one wanted to believe and what was true often weren't the same thing. God knew, he should have learned that lesson long ago. He'd had enough teachers.

He glanced at Alyson. Her forehead knotted with worry. Her lips tightened into a line.

Following Dex's gaze, Cohen watched her, as well. ''Sorry to disappoint you, Alyson. But I guess I'm not as bad a guy as you thought.''

She shook her head. ''It's not that, John. We just need to find out who did help him.''

''Hmm. Maybe I can help, after all.''

Dex tensed. He leaned over the table. ''Spit it out, Cohen.''

''There was a hearing for the jail assault case a week ago, and I had to spring Smythe for a day to testify. He had a girlfriend in the gallery. At least, she seemed like a girlfriend, smiling at him, lots of eye contact when he was on the stand. Sick woman.''

''Who was she?''

''That's the interesting part. I ran into her one other time this week. She testified in one of my cases. Her name is Jennifer Scott.''

Alyson gasped.

Dex turned to her. "Do you know Jennifer Scott?"

Alyson nodded and swallowed hard, as if trying to find the courage to face something she didn't want to face. "She's a forensic chemist. She works with me at the crime lab."

"HAVEN'T YOU HEARD?" Valerie D'Fonse looked down her generous nose at Alyson, a conspiratorial grin on her face.

Alyson wasn't in the mood for guessing games. Last night had been hell. She'd spent it in Dex's guest room again after he'd refused to let her stay in her home until a security system was installed. She'd have rather stayed alone. He hadn't said two words to her all night. He'd merely retreated into his library with the telephone. So much for his promise not to shut her out.

She bit the inside of her bottom lip. She didn't know if she could stand one more night without Patrick safe in her arms. She needed answers. And fast. She'd come straight to Valerie for just that reason.

A brilliant but lonely forensic chemist, Valerie had made other people's business her hobby. She spewed gossip the way Fourth of July fireworks spewed sparks. And that's why Alyson was circulating in the crime lab's break room to learn what she could learn. "I'm so out of the loop, Valerie. I haven't heard anything. What happened?"

Valerie's eyes sparkled as if all the gossip she packed into her mind was gunpowder and by asking the question, Alyson had just set flame to fuse. "Jennifer Scott doesn't work here anymore."

Alyson's heart plummeted. "Why not?"

"She quit two days ago. Didn't even give notice."

"Two days ago?" How coincidental that Jennifer should quit the very day Smythe was released from prison. "No notice?"

"Not a peep. *I* didn't even know she was going to quit. But that's not the good part." She lowered her voice and leaned toward Alyson over a table littered with candy wrappers and a paper bag lunch. "You'll never guess where she got a job."

Back to guessing games again. "Where?"

"Think big company, lots of bucks. And they don't hand out jobs like candy at a parade. Let's just say she must have an in."

"Where, Valerie? Where did Jennifer get a job?"

Valerie grinned, her whole body tensed with the excitement of being the keeper of gossip in demand. "Smythe Pharmaceuticals."

The name hit Alyson like a well-aimed fist. Now they were getting somewhere.

DEX COULD TELL Alyson had news the moment she poked her head into her lab where he was sitting in front of her computer, waiting for her. Her eyes sparkled like emeralds under a jeweler's glass. Her cheeks flushed with color. The way she used to look, back when their biggest troubles were deciding which restaurant to choose among the dozens flanking State Street.

So different from the drawn look of fear she'd worn for the past few days.

She motioned him across the hall and into the vacant trace evidence lab and shut the door behind them, leaning back against the barrier.

"So?"

"Jennifer Scott quit two days ago. She has a new job."

The news zinged along his nerves like an electric charge. "Don't tell me. Her new job is with Smythe Pharmaceuticals."

"Bingo."

Dex reached into his pocket and pulled out his cell phone. "Do you have a number for them?"

Alyson nodded. She disappeared from the lab for a few moments then reappeared with the Madison phone book.

Dex paged through the thick book to locate the number and punched it into his phone.

"Smythe Pharmaceuticals," a professional-sounding woman's voice answered.

"I'd like to speak with Jennifer Scott, please."

A pause stretched over the line. "I'm sorry, there's no one here by that name."

"Are you saying a chemist by the name of Jennifer Scott doesn't work there?"

"That's right, sir."

"Thank you." Dex punched the end button and slipped the phone back into his jacket pocket. "Damn. Is your gossip guru known for inventing stories?"

Alyson watched him, the sparkle gone from her eyes, a furrow between her delicate brows. "No. Usually she just sticks to repeating them. But why would Jennifer tell Valerie she had a job at Smythe Pharmaceuticals if she didn't?" Alyson stuffed her hands into her pockets. "Unless Jennifer expected to be offered the job but the offer never came."

"We won't know until we find her."

"So now we have two missing persons. Jennifer Scott and the alleged rape victim, Connie Rasula."

He nodded. "That's what it looks like."

"I suppose we'd better get looking." She turned and grasped the doorknob, but didn't pull it open. "Wait."

"What is it?"

She spun to face Dex, the sparkle back in her eyes. "Maybe we don't have to find Jennifer to learn whether she stole that sample of Smythe's blood from the crime lab."

"I'm listening."

"When we take a blood sample for DNA or serum testing, we have to add a preservative to it so the liquid blood doesn't coagulate and start to decompose like blood normally would. The preservative is called E.D.T.A."

The name of the chemical rang a bell in Dex's memory. It had made the news during the O.J. Simpson case. "Isn't E.D.T.A. present in blood naturally?"

"Only in trace amounts introduced by preserved food or other household products. But the blood sample taken from Smythe by the lab will have a very high E.D.T.A. content. If Jennifer stole blood from the lab sample, the blood found under the recent rape victim's fingernails will have an equally high E.D.T.A. content."

Dex nodded. "And if the blood is the result of the victim clawing the rapist in self-defense as the victim claims, there should be only trace amounts of E.D.T.A. present."

"Trace amounts at most."

"How long will testing take?"

Alyson pursed her lips together like she always did when doing mental calculations. "If we get a specialist who's used to doing the testing and you put a little clout behind the request, I'd say we could have results in about a day."

He couldn't stop a grin from spreading over his lips. "Set it up."

"I'll ready the sample myself. And I'll label the samples anonymous."

"Good thinking."

Alyson shot him a triumphant smile that hit him like a punch to the gut. He used to burst with pride at the thought of having this brilliant woman in his life, in his bed. Whenever she made a contribution to a case, or found the answer to a tough problem as she had just now, he'd always felt like crowing.

He mentally shook his head. He no longer had a reason to be proud. Alyson wasn't his anymore. If he hadn't wanted to truly face that before, he had only to remind himself of the baby she'd hid from him.

He had to remember. He had to hold on to the anger, the hurt. He couldn't let himself forget. He had learned that early in life.

He glanced at his watch. The day was trickling away.

Alyson opened the door to the evidence lab. "Hi, Valerie." She smiled at a dark-haired woman and waited for her to walk past before stepping into the hall. She turned back to glance at Dex. "It'll just take me a few minutes to get the testing under way."

"So it should be complete by—" The bleat of Dex's cell phone cut off his thought. He retrieved it from his pocket and punched the button. "Harrington."

"Got some news." Al Mylinski's voice boomed over the phone.

"What kind of news, Mylinski?"

"Important news. I'll meet you in your office."

"Will do." Dex punched off the phone and met Alyson's concerned gaze. "We have to go to my office. Mylinski has news."

Chapter Five

Alyson fought to keep her breathing measured, her pulse rate under control as she and Dex rode the elevator to the fifth floor of the City County Building. There was only one reason Dex would have insisted she accompany him to the D.A.'s offices. If he merely wanted to protect her from Smythe, he could have left her at the crime lab with no worry. And he would have if Al Mylinski's call pertained to a case she had no business hearing about. No, this had something to do with Patrick.

Questions echoed through her mind. Had the police located their son? Was he all right? Or was the news much worse? Was it the unthinkable?

Taking a firm grip on the panic screaming along her nerves, she followed Dex down the hall and into the reception area. The place looked just as it had when her father was in charge, government-beige walls, Spartan furniture, a far cry from the richly appointed offices of private attorneys. These lawyers worked for the public, and it showed.

Maggie Daugherty shuffled papers behind the counter as she always had when Fitz was alive. With one difference. Instead of greeting Alyson with a big smile, she avoided Alyson's gaze, a guarded look in her saucer-size brown eyes.

Dex paused at the desk. "Is Al Mylinski here yet, Maggie?"

She motioned down the hall. "He's waiting in your office."

"Hold my calls."

The receptionist gave him a tense smile. "Certainly, Mr. Harrington." Her head dipped back to her work.

Dex motioned to Alyson to follow and strode back into the maze of halls. Reaching the door of his office, he opened it and ushered her inside.

Stepping into the office, she braced herself. But the blow of memory she expected never came. The walnut desk her father had used had been replaced by a sturdy oak one. The leather chairs were gone, as well, an inexpensive vinyl taking their place. Even the art had changed. Instead of classic paintings of landscapes, modern prints brightened the walls. Dex had wiped Fitz's presence from the room as effectively as he'd wiped her presence from his house. And while the absence of memories was a relief, it also left her cold inside.

And alone.

"Alyson. What a nice surprise." Resting his heavy-set frame in one of the chairs facing Dex's desk, Al Mylinski focused on her.

A shiver of fear worked its way up her spine. She'd always liked Al. His dry sense of humor and shrewd blue eyes along with his excellent police work had earned her affection and respect the few times she'd worked on his cases at the lab or run into him at her father's or Dex's offices. And he seemed to be truly happy to see her. But for the life of her, she couldn't force a real smile to her lips. "Why did you call, Al? What happened?"

Mylinski glanced at Dex, as if asking his permission to speak in front of her.

Dex nodded. "Go ahead. What have you found?" Propping a hip on the edge of his desk, he waited for Mylinski's answer.

"Looks like our alleged rape victim is up north. Her family has a cabin near Minocqua. The family's housekeeper thinks our girl has been living there the past few months."

Panic surged along Alyson's nerves. Smythe's warnings not to involve the police rang in her ears. "No." She whirled to face Dex. "No police. He said no police."

Dex held up his hands as if warding off her assault. "I didn't call Mylinski about Patrick. He's been working on finding Connie Rasula since she disappeared. His involvement has nothing to do with Patrick.''

''It has everything to do with Patrick. What if Smythe finds out?''

''You've heard from Smythe?'' Al glanced from Alyson to Dex and back again, taking in far more than she wanted him to.

Alyson shot Dex a concerned glare.

Dex looked away and focused on Mylinski. ''Smythe kidnapped our son.''

''And he warned you not to involve the cops,'' Mylinski supplied.

''That's right.''

Mylinski dug into his pocket and popped a piece of orange candy into his mouth. He bit down on the candy and ground it between his teeth as he processed the information. His sharp gaze traveled from Alyson to Dex and back again. ''Since when did you two have a son anyway? Or shouldn't I ask?''

The scent of orange filled the room, turning Alyson's stomach. ''Dex just learned about him two days ago. He's seven months old. His name is Patrick.''

A crooked smile spread over Mylinski's lips. ''Well, congratulations. And if there's anything I can do behind the scenes to nail that bastard and bring your baby back, count me in.''

''We'll drive up north and talk to Connie Rasula

today." Dex glanced at Alyson. "But I do have another missing person."

"Just give me a name," Mylinski said.

"Jennifer Scott. Until two days ago she was a chemist at the State Crime Lab," Dex offered.

Mylinski's brow furrowed. He steepled his fingers and tapped them against his lips. "Jennifer Scott. Mid-thirties, blond hair, average size, lives alone in a nice condo out in Fitchburg?"

Dex leaned back against his desk as if bracing himself. "What do you know?"

"Her mother is a friend of mine. I talked to her this morning. She came in and filled out a missing person's report. Her daughter was supposed to meet her two days ago and never showed. Hasn't been heard from since."

Dread grasped the back of Alyson's neck like a cold hand. "Smythe was let out of prison two days ago."

Dex nodded. "And I doubt we're talking about a coincidence here. Not where Smythe is concerned."

First Connie Rasula was missing, then Patrick, and now Jennifer Scott. No. No coincidence. Alyson could feel it.

THE INVIGORATING SCENT of pine trees and crisp air rushed through the open car window and hit Dex's face like a cool splash of aftershave. Beside him in the passenger seat, Alyson pulled out a Wisconsin map. She'd watched as the freeway had dwindled to a highway and finally to a country road. Apparently she wasn't taking any chances on ending up lost in the north woods.

They'd driven most of the four-hour trip in silence—a silence for which Dex had been grateful. Too many ugly scenarios were spinning through his mind. The fate of Jennifer Scott; what they would find when they located Connie Rasula; and most of all, where was Patrick?

And then there was Alyson herself. The sparkle he had seen in her eyes at the lab had long since been extinguished. Lines of tension surrounded her pursed lips. Her fingers gripped the map as if it were a lifeline. No doubt the same horrible scenarios were plaguing her, as well.

He returned his gaze to the road. He couldn't think about how Alyson felt right now. If he did, he'd only want to take her in his arms, to comfort her, to reassure her that everything would be all right. He had to focus on finding Connie Rasula. He had to convince her to tell everything she knew—about the false rape that sprung Smythe from prison, about the rapist's plans for revenge, and about Patrick's whereabouts. She was the only lead they had.

The winding country road widened, hotels and resorts began springing up along the shores of pristine lakes. Traffic increased. And the sparsely populated area turned into a resort town, complete with gift shops, gourmet restaurants and luxury hotels. Overweight people wandered from shop to eatery, baring their shockingly white legs in shorts and dresses. And somewhere among the tourists was the woman they were looking for. The woman they had to find.

The address Mylinski had given him was still folded in Dex's wallet, but he didn't have to slip it out to remember. He'd burned the street and number into his memory the first time he'd glanced at them. He had only to get through town and find the right road circling the lake, then Connie Rasula and some answers would be his.

They reached the Rasula summer home just as the sun was starting to slip beyond the bluffs on the other side of the lake. The orange of the sun's rays reflected on the water, turning the waves into tongues of fire. The home itself was bigger than some of the hotels in town. A rough-hewn cabin design, the house seemed to have more windows than logs. Alyson followed Dex up the curved walkway amid the blooms of perennials and colorful bushes. He mounted the front steps and pressed the doorbell.

The chime sounded through the house, echoing as if inside a church. They waited, but there seemed to be no movement on the other side of the door.

Dex punched the doorbell again. Still no response. He tried jiggling the knob, but it didn't move. The place was securely locked. "Damn."

"Maybe she went out for dinner or something."

"Maybe." He hoped her absence was something so innocent, so ordinary. But the tension winding up his spine suggested something different.

"You think something is wrong?" Alyson's eyes searched his as if desperate for an answer.

He sure as hell hoped not. "She's probably just out eating dinner, like you said." Trying not to let Alyson read his eyes, he walked down the steps and headed around the side of the house. He wasn't going to give up this easily. Connie could have recognized him. She could be hiding inside the house, waiting until they left. But whatever the explanation, he wanted to know more before they gave up and found a hotel for the night.

Alyson followed close behind. They circled the house to the lake side. The ground sloped to the water. The house rose above them in three stories of glass and wood decking. A lakeside paradise.

Dex started up the steps leading to the tiered deck, Alyson on his heels. Tall pines stabbed into the sky on either side of them. The lake yawned like a black hole beneath them, waves tainted by the blue glow of twilight. Their footsteps thumped on the wooden stairs like an irregular heartbeat.

They reached the first level of decking. Dex moved to the sliding-glass doors. Shielding the reflected glow of the horizon behind him with his hand, he peered inside. Alyson caught up to him and did the same.

Pristine-white carpet and furniture scattered the living room. Dark shadows cloaked the hallways and kitchen beyond. But other than a half-full wine-glass perched on the coffee table and an open magazine, there was no sign of life.

"It doesn't look like anyone is home." Alyson tried the door handle. It rattled, but didn't budge. "So what do we do now?"

Dex turned and headed for the stairs before the question had cleared her lips. "There's one more floor. Maybe we'll get lucky." He reached the stairs, his footsteps pounding out a rhythm as he started for the top deck.

The shadows grew deeper the higher they climbed. Tops of trees swayed in the breeze. Finally they reached the top deck, taller than all but the tallest pines. Light was fading fast from the sky. Long shadows deepened and spread over the deck, obscuring flowerpots and redwood furniture. Dex walked straight for one of the sliding-glass doors stretching the length of the deck.

Alyson dodged through a clutter of outdoor furniture obviously on her way to the windows stretching along the other side of the deck. Suddenly her footsteps stopped. "Dex." Her voice rasped as if her throat was being squeezed by a strong hand.

Dex spun around.

Her eyes were wide against her pale face. Her chest rose and fell with rapid breaths. She swallowed and looked down at her feet.

Dex followed her gaze to the shadowed form on the deck and looked into the glassy eyes of Connie Rasula.

Chapter Six

"We have to call the police." Alyson's voice rang in her own ears. Panic jangled through her, yet her voice sounded flat and emotionless, her emotions kept in line by sheer force of will.

Dex knelt and touched his fingers to the woman's neck. "She's dead." Under his fingers, the bruises on her neck were dark blue and red, visible even in the dark shadow. They looked like the mottled outline of hands rather than the dark, precise line of a ligature. However, her wrists had clearly been tied, dark bruised lines dug deep into the fragile flesh. And from the waist down, she was naked.

Anger and repulsion swirled in Alyson's head until she was dizzy. "Smythe."

Dex rose to his feet. "Apparently he learned one thing from his time in prison. Not to leave live witnesses."

Alyson's gaze darted around the deck to the dark interior of the cabin. Anywhere but at the body inches in front of her feet. "Do you think he's here?"

Dex shook his head. "Her body is cool and rigor has set in."

"She must have been dead for a while then." Alyson gasped for breath, but she couldn't seem to scoop enough oxygen into her hungry lungs. Her head began to whirl, and for a moment she feared she might pass out.

Dex grasped her elbow and led her away from the body. "Smythe has no reason to hurt Patrick. He needs him for leverage. He needs him in order to exert control over us. Over me."

Alyson nodded, but her head wouldn't stop spinning. Her heart wouldn't stop pounding. Tears welled in her eyes and spilled over her lashes.

Dex wrapped an arm around her and pulled her against his body. "Patrick will be all right. We won't let anything happen to him."

Alyson couldn't stop shaking, couldn't stop tears from coursing down her cheeks. She'd tried so hard to be strong. But she couldn't do it anymore. She couldn't physically do it.

Dex grasped her chin and turned her face to his. His eyes drilled into her. "This has been hard for you. Harder than I can imagine. But you have to hold on. We'll get through this."

She tried to raise her chin and straighten her

spine, but the tremor racking her body wouldn't allow it. "I'm okay."

"Like hell you are."

He was right. She couldn't breathe. She couldn't think. It was as if walls were closing in on her, walls she couldn't see. Cutting off her air. Trapping her in terrible isolation.

Dex pulled her closer. His solidness, his warmth, broke down the walls. She wanted to be close to him, the father of her baby, the only human being feeling the same fear she felt.

The man she'd once loved.

They stood that way for a long while. And even though he was only holding her out of pity, out of concern, she could almost bring herself to believe that he was here with her, holding her because he cared about her. That she wasn't so alone.

And that was enough. That was everything.

She looked up into his eyes. "We have to go."

"I doubt that Smythe is still here. He's too smart to risk being seen near Connie Rasula. Especially now that she's dead."

"It's not that. I just have this horrible feeling." She clutched Dex's shirt in her fingers to still her shaking hands. "Now that Smythe has covered his tracks, I'm afraid he's ready to make his next move."

Dex narrowed his eyes on her and nodded. "I think you're probably right." He pulled out his cell phone and punched 9-1-1. "The sooner we report this, the sooner we can get on the highway back to Madison."

Alyson watched as he calmly reported the murder. But he didn't pull away from her. And she couldn't bring herself to break contact with him, either. Not now. Not yet. She needed his touch, his strength, to get through the next few hours. And somehow he must have recognized it.

Or maybe he needed it, too.

THE CAR'S TIRES hummed along the highway, snaking through the towering pine trees and darkness ahead. Dex gripped the wheel with one hand and slugged back hot coffee with the other. He didn't need the caffeine to stay awake. Not after all they'd weathered this evening—discovering Connie Rasula's body, fielding endless questions from the local police. His mind was humming louder than the vehicle's spinning tires. But the coffee was warm and reassuring, and it filled the car with its rich aroma. A touch of normalcy in a day that had spun so out of control.

And if by some chance the fatigue of emotionally charged days and sleepless nights overcame the caffeine and seized control of his body, he had only to glance at the passenger seat next to him, where Alyson sat, her wide green eyes staring straight ahead,

her auburn hair wisping around her shoulders, and
his blood would jolt him back to rigid attention.

He could still feel the press of her body against
him. The way her sweet curves fit him. The way the
fear in her eyes and the trembling of her flesh made
him want to hold her and comfort her and never let
her go.

He forced himself to focus on the darkness just
beyond the glow of the headlights. He'd been so in
love with her once, more in love than he'd ever believed he could be. But it had all been a fantasy.
The last streak of romantic idealism to be snuffed
out. Now he needed to keep himself anchored in
reality. Alyson hadn't trusted him. He couldn't forget that. She'd chosen to believe her father over him.
And worst of all, she'd kept their baby from him.

His baby.

He hadn't let himself think of Patrick since he'd
learned he had a baby—and that baby had been stolen. He hadn't had the time or the luxury of thinking,
of feeling. He'd focused on tracking down Smythe.
On fixing the problem. But in the dark car, his imagination swirled around him like a chilling fog.

His baby.

He used to think about having children. Of how
he'd make damn sure he was a good father, a good
provider, unlike his worthless old man. He'd even
lain awake some nights wondering exactly how he

would go about fatherhood—considering his lack of role model.

But all that changed when Alyson betrayed him and their relationship ended. Without a wife, he had no reason to contemplate being a father. At least, that's what he had believed.

And now, low and behold, he had a son. A son he might never know.

He glanced at Alyson despite himself. Posture rigid, she stared into the night as if facing her worst fears. Her arms wrapped around her middle as though if she held on tightly enough, she could keep from shattering into a million pieces.

It was hell for her, losing her son. Dex knew that. But he couldn't help envying her nonetheless. At least she knew what she'd lost. She knew what Patrick's little body felt like snuggled against her breast. She knew how his little face lit up when he laughed or what funny noises made him smile. Dex might never know those things. He might never know his son.

And that made him saddest of all. "Tell me about him. Tell me about Patrick." His voice sounded flat over the hum of the tires. He was more empty and tired than he was aware he was feeling.

Alyson's face jerked in his direction.

"I need to know." He forced a note of gentleness into his voice. "Tell me about my son."

Alyson's eyes glowed in the green light of the

dash. She searched his face for what seemed like an eternity. Finally she took a deep breath. "He was born on a Thursday afternoon." Her lips lifted at the corners. Her eyes took on a faraway look. "I went through thirty-five hours of labor, and I was so tired I truly thought I wasn't going to make it. But when I first saw him, none of it mattered."

From the look on her face, he knew it wasn't just the pain and exhaustion of labor she was referring to. But the torment she'd lived through after her father's death. And the stress of having a baby alone. "I should have been there."

"I know. I'm sorry." She dipped her head as if hiding the tears he knew misted her eyes.

Damn. Even though his absence hadn't been his choice, he still felt guilty. Guilt he had no reason to feel. He hadn't abandoned her. *She'd* stolen those moments, those memories, from him. He had the right to be angry about that.

Just as he had the right to know about his son now. "Tell me more."

"He looks so much like you. Even when he was just born—with that red little face and pointed head newborns have." She raised her chin and stared at the highway, not bothering to wipe the tears that clung to her lower lashes. "The first thing I noticed was the little cleft in his chin. Just like yours."

Dex ran a finger over his chin, feeling the dent he had passed to his son.

"He was born with black hair, but now he's a little towhead. A blonde, just like you. Not a hint of my red hair."

Something welled up inside him, something akin to pride. "So he really looks like me?"

"Spitting image. Down to the blue eyes and square jaw." The hint of a smile tugged at the corners of her lips. Her eyes softened, transforming her face into the picture of proud motherhood. "But he has my temperament."

"Probably a good thing. You're the most even-tempered Irish redhead on the planet."

"That's not saying much."

"Maybe not. But it sure as hell is better than him taking after my side of the family." He didn't have to try very hard to remember the hard lash of his father's temper, when he cared enough to leave the tavern and deal with his son at all. Drunk or sober, the old man was a worthless bastard of the first order. And although by some miracle Dex didn't seem to have inherited the old man's violent outbursts, no one would peg him as the forgiving sort. "What else can you tell me about him?"

She turned her gaze back to the highway, deep in thought. "He's always been a good baby. He had no trouble eating. He slept through the night when he was only two months old. And he's strong. He can pull himself into standing position already. And don't let him grab the spoon when you're feeding him, or you'll never get it back.''

''So he's a strapping little guy, huh?''

''Yup. But he's cuddly, too. Sometimes when he's had enough action, he curls up in my arms and sleeps like a little angel.'' Her voice ached with love, with tenderness, with a thousand memories of moments with a child Dex might never know.

He swallowed into a raw throat and concentrated on the road ahead. He had every right to be furious with Alyson for keeping their son from him. But somehow he couldn't manage it. Anger eluded him. And he was left with nothing but regret. ''I wish I knew him. I wish I'd been part of his life. I wish I'd been there.''

Alyson closed her eyes. ''I wish you'd been there, too.''

BIRDS HAD BEGUN their early morning songs by the time Alyson and Dex climbed out of his car in the driveway of his bungalow. Except for a short stop at home to pick up clothing and toiletries, she hadn't set foot in her little Cape Cod since the night Smythe had taken Patrick. Just thinking of the empty bedroom—the room Patrick's soft baby scent used to fill—she winced. The thought of venturing back into her house, of imagining Smythe's eyes staring at her from the darkness of predawn, made her mouth go dry. ''Thanks for letting me stay here. I don't know what I'd do at home waiting for Smythe to show up with his chloroform and rope."

"You don't have to worry about that anymore."

"Why not?" After Dex's warnings and the way he'd stuck by her side to protect her, she never would have expected those words from his lips.

"The security company left a message for me at the office. They've finally installed that alarm system in your house. I'll take you home tomorrow."

Alyson nodded, trying to look grateful. And braver than she felt. A security system was nice, but it still didn't make her feel safe. Not really. What did it matter if the thing screeched to high heaven if Smythe was already in the house coming after her? "Thanks, Dex. I appreciate it."

"Smythe never would have targeted you if it wasn't for your relationship with me. The least I can do is insure your safety. I've also talked to Mylinski about setting up some undercover officers to watch your house."

A chill shot up her spine. "No."

"They would be in an unmarked car and plain clothes. No one would know they're cops."

"Except Smythe. You heard him, Dex. He has sources. Maybe in the police department itself. He said he'd know if we got the police involved. I'm not taking the chance."

Although a muscle clenched along his jaw, he didn't argue. "All right. No police outside your

house. But if an intruder sets off the alarm, the police will be there in minutes.''

She blew a stream of air through pursed lips. The
hard lines of his jaw told her there would be no use
arguing this point. Truth be told, she didn't want to
argue. If Smythe came after her, she wanted the police to be on their way. Then they could arrest him
and find out where he'd hidden Patrick.

''It's all set then. I'll take you home tomorrow.
Depending on what Smythe does, we'll decide what
to do from there.''

A chill skittered over her skin, but she managed
a nod. She didn't want to face the empty rooms in
her house—rooms Smythe had violated with his
presence—but she couldn't expect Dex to baby-sit
her, either. She forced her chin up a notch. ''Okay.
Tomorrow.''

''You don't want to be alone, do you?''

She started. Dex had always been able to look
into her heart, to read her thoughts and feelings.
Many things had changed between them, but that
wasn't one of them. ''No. I keep thinking of that
empty house, those empty rooms.''

''And remembering Smythe's attack.''

She nodded and looked away. The scent of chloroform lingered in her mind along with the sharp
edge of fear.

''Forget going home tomorrow. You can stay here
as long as you like.''

A shock traveled up Alyson's spine at his offer. First the tenderness he'd shown after they'd found Connie Rasula's body, then his wish in the car, and now this.

Dex was a hard man. An unforgiving man. She knew that better than most people. She'd seen it in his work. She'd felt it firsthand. But his tenderness now, his apparent concern for her, the way his anger had dissolved into warmth for the son he'd never met and by extension for her, caught her off guard.

She looked into his face, so sincere, so serious, so like the man she'd fallen in love with. Tearing her gaze away, she focused on the front door. Pre-dawn birdsong jangled around her, echoing the chaos that pounded inside her.

He unlocked the door and ushered her into the house. "Do you want something to eat?"

They hadn't eaten since downing a doughnut and coffee at a truck stop along the interstate. Not exactly a bonanza of nutrition. But despite the fact that she should be famished, the thought of food turned her stomach. "No, thanks. I think I'll just go to bed."

"Smart choice. The sun will be coming up in about an hour. We'd better get some sleep while we can."

Dex hadn't said the words, but she knew what he meant. *Before Smythe makes his next move.*

She started up the stairs toward the guest room at

the end of the hall. Dex's house was large, rambling, but even though he was sleeping on a different floor and on the opposite side of the house, she could feel him in the house with her. And she knew she wasn't alone.

Unlike Patrick. Unlike her baby who was who knew where.

Tears surged at the backs of her eyes. Questions shuddered through her mind. Was her little boy alone? Had someone rocked him and sung songs to him? Had someone kissed his forehead and tucked him into bed the way she did every night?

Was someone taking care of him?

She gripped the wood banister and tried to steady herself.

"We'll find him, Alyson. And then you won't have to worry about Patrick or about Smythe attacking you. We'll find him and get him back. And then you won't be alone anymore."

She looked down where Dex stood at the bottom of the stairs, his face blurred by her tears. Maybe he could still read her thoughts, but he'd missed one thing. Her fear of being alone hadn't started the night Smythe had attacked her and kidnapped Patrick. It had started over a year ago, when Dex walked out of her life.

ANDY SMYTHE leaned back in the seat of his rented sedan. The car was a piece of junk, but he couldn't risk someone spotting his Corvette. Not up in the northwoods boondocks and not tonight.

He scanned the quiet, oak-lined street. Though painted different colors, the small, square houses looked as if a builder had produced them with a cookie cutter. Even the bushes rimming each house's aluminum siding looked the same. The only difference was the light glowing from the windows of the house Andy watched. The neighbors had the good sense to be asleep already. Not the man inside.

A police detective's hours.

Not that Andy didn't know all about sleepless nights. Thanks to that bastard Harrington, he hadn't gotten a decent night's sleep since the day that damn jury pronounced him guilty. Never mind that the bitches he'd attacked had deserved it. Some of the whores had probably even liked it.

Well, none of that mattered anymore. He'd already started paying Harrington back. And he wouldn't quit until the man was destroyed. And then, if he was feeling particularly charitable, he would put Harrington out of his misery. For good.

The light dimmed and finally switched off.

It was about damn time. Andy glanced at his Rolex. He'd wait a half hour before making his move. A half hour would give the cop inside plenty of chance to fall into a nice, deep sleep.

A sleep he'd never wake up from.

Andy leaned back in the seat of his rented junker

and smiled. He could have hired someone to take care of this. Just shelled out the cash and gotten the job done, like his old man liked to do. Of course the old man didn't kill anyone. Not that Andy knew of, anyway. He just paid people to take care of his business obligations. And to keep his family out of his hair. But the old man didn't understand one important thing. Some things were much better when you did them yourself. And, as Andy had discovered with the Rasula bitch, murder was one of them.

He closed his eyes, reliving the way he'd put her in her place, the way he'd punished her, the way he'd choked the life from her when he was finished. He only wished he would have realized how pleasurable murder could be years ago. If he'd known then what he knew now, he'd never have let those bitches live. Harrington never would have been able to parade their pitiful, whining stories in front of the jury. And Andy wouldn't have spent one hour behind bars.

He looked down at his Rolex again and watched the last minutes of the detective's life tick away. This murder was also Harrington's fault. Smythe had made it clear to the redhead that they weren't to involve the cops. But Harrington had to get cocky. He had to ignore Andy's demands. He'd probably figured that Andy would never find out.

Guess again.

He pulled a black ski mask over his head. Pushing

open the door of his car, he stepped out onto the shadowed street. He walked quickly across the neighbor's lawn to the little green box house on the corner. Circling the property, he plunged into a thicket of bushes near the bedroom window.

Once in the shadow of the bushes, he dipped his hand into his sweatshirt pocket and withdrew the .38 he'd picked up from a Chicago drug dealer. He attached the little silencer and sidled up to the window. The gun fit his palm as though it belonged there.

A thrill scuttled over his nerves. A feeling of strength. There was nothing as potent as holding the power of life and death in your hands. As long as you had the guts to use it. Andy had the power, and now he had the guts, too. Prison had hardened him, that was for sure. And Harrington and the redhead would feel that hard edge. And Detective Al Mylinski would feel it as well, with the sharpness of a bullet to the heart.

They would all wish they had listened to Andy Smythe.

Chapter Seven

Dex jolted upright. He ripped the blanket from around his legs and sprang to his feet. Something had awakened him, a sound, but what? Sunlight peeked around the wood-slat blinds covering his bedroom windows. A cacophony of birdsong clattered outside overriding the lap of waves. But it wasn't the sun or the birds that had awakened him. It was something else.

The distant chirp of a cell phone rose over the birdsong.

The phone. Alyson's phone. *Smythe.*

Heart slamming against his rib cage, Dex pulled his pants on and ran for the staircase. He took the steps two at a time and raced down the hall. Reaching the open door of the guest bedroom, he plunged inside.

Alyson sat in the bed. Auburn hair tousled in sleep, she stared at him, green eyes wide. The sheet pooled around her waist, exposing a silk nightie that barely covered her full breasts.

The phone rang again.

As if the sound had jolted her out of a trance, Alyson grabbed the cell phone out of her purse on the bedside table and punched the button. "Hello?" Her face blanched.

Dex crossed the room to her side. Damn. Since the call was on the cell phone, there was no way to record it. Or trace it. The best they could do was find out the general area the phone call originated. Not that it would do them much good.

"What do you want us to do?" Alyson listened carefully, gathering the sheet around her as if she were chilled. "No. You can't ask him to do that."

Dex held out his hand for the phone. "Tell the bastard if he plans to demand something of me, he's going to have to do it directly."

Meeting Dex's eyes, Alyson handed him the phone with a shaking hand.

He held it to his ear. "What do you want, Smythe?"

"So the redhead is staying with you. I should have known. Did you get lucky?"

"Go to hell."

"I've already been there, Harrington. And you're the one who sent me."

"What do you want?"

"I want to return the favor. We'll start with you holding a press conference. Tomorrow."

"What the hell is this about?"

"You're going to do the county a favor and resign your job. But that's not all. I want a public apology. I want you to tell whoever will listen that you were malicious in your conviction of me. And that I am innocent."

Cold rage pounded in Dex's ears. "Like hell I will."

Smythe's laugh rumbled low, like approaching thunder. "He's a cute kid, Harrington. I'd hate to see anything happen to him."

Dex grasped the phone until the plastic creaked in his fist.

Alyson watched him with wide eyes. She looked so small in the wide bed surrounded by white sheets. So unguarded and vulnerable.

He wanted to reach out to her, to comfort her, to repeat the assurances he'd given her last night. But in the light of day, he wasn't sure if his words would ring true. He wasn't sure of anything at all. Whatever reassurances he gave her would be a lie.

"And there's another thing."

"What?" Dex growled through clenched teeth.

"When I talked to the redhead, I told her I didn't want the police involved."

"The police aren't involved."

"If it looks like a cop and squawks like a cop,

chances are it's too close to being a cop for my tastes.''

An uneasy feeling crept up Dex's spine. "What are you getting at, Smythe?"

"A little bird told me a detective has been poking his nose where it doesn't belong. Imagine that. And after I warned you against involving the cops."

Damn. He had to be referring to Mylinski. How the hell did Smythe know Mylinski had been helping them? "We've been looking for Connie Rasula since she disappeared right after she reported being raped. But I pulled the detective off the case."

"That's not the way I heard it. Now why would you lie to me? Don't you realize this is serious? Don't you realize I have your baby—that I can kill him if I want to? Don't you realize you're not in charge anymore?"

"Take it easy, Smythe. I'm talking to you on the phone, aren't I? I'm listening to what you have to say."

"That's not enough. But don't worry. Since you failed to pull your cop off the case, I did it for you."

Dex's throat tightened. "What did you do?"

Smythe chuckled on the other end of the line. "First you caused Connie Rasula's unfortunate demise and now a police detective's. Maybe next time you'll listen to me."

"What the hell did you do?" Dex's pulse thundered in his ears. But Smythe merely laughed again, until a click sounded on the line, harsh and final.

Dex sank to the bed and let the phone fall into his lap.

Alyson scrambled across the bed to his side. She grasped his arm. "What happened? What did he say?"

Dex looked at her. His mind raced, searching for an answer he could give. An answer he could accept.

"What did he say, Dex?" Alyson's eyes widened with fear. "Did he say something about Patrick?"

Dex managed to shake his head. "Not Patrick. Mylinski."

Alyson gasped. "He found out Al located Connie Rasula?"

"Yes."

"What did he do?"

Images bombarded him. Mylinski's bloody body in a ditch. Or charred beyond recognition in his car. Or lying in a Dumpster with a slit throat. Dex gritted his teeth. He'd had it with guessing games. He needed answers. He punched Al's cell number into the phone.

Alyson watched him, her bottom lip clamped between her teeth, her fingers digging into the flesh of his arm.

The phone rang in Dex's ear. No answer.

He disconnected the call, punched in 9-1-1 and turned to Alyson. "Get dressed. Hurry."

DEX PACED the floor of the ICU waiting room. He and Alyson had reached Mylinski's house just as the paramedics had carried Al Mylinski out of the front door on a stretcher. They'd found him in bed, shot several times through a nearby window. He'd been bleeding badly, barely clinging to life when he'd reached the hospital. The doctors had rushed him into surgery. Now there was nothing they could do but wait.

And pray.

"It's not your fault, Dex. You know that, don't you?" Alyson's voice washed over him.

He'd felt her eyes on him since the moment they'd discovered exactly what Smythe had done to Mylinski. She'd been trying to read his thoughts, to gauge his emotions. She needn't bother. "You might as well save your breath. It's not going to work."

"What isn't going to work?"

"Your attempt to keep me from feeling guilty. I should have asked the police to discontinue the search for Connie Rasula the moment Smythe made his demands."

"How do you know they would have done what you asked? What reason would you have given them?"

She had a point. As district attorney he worked in partnership with the police, but he wasn't exactly in a position to give orders. And he couldn't have told

Mylinski's superiors about Patrick, not without involving the sheriff's department, a move that would have raised Smythe's ire tenfold. "I should have done something. If I had, Mylinski wouldn't be fighting for his life now. I can't fool myself."

"I'm not asking you to. I just think you shouldn't be so hard on yourself."

He gritted his teeth and kept up his relentless pace. If anything was worse than his own guilt echoing in his ears, it was Alyson's charity. "Listen, I appreciate you trying to support me, but I don't need it."

"I think you do. You just don't want to take it."

Maybe not. Maybe it reminded him too much of the support and love and trust he'd once thought was between them. Maybe it made him want to believe those things could be between them again. "I'll be fine. It's Mylinski you should be worrying about. Not me."

Footsteps approached from down the hall. Dex spun in the direction of the sound. A young-looking man in blue scrubs stepped into the waiting room. Circles hung under the man's wide brown eyes, making them look as droopy as a bloodhound's. He leveled a serious stare on Dex. "Are you waiting to hear about Alfred Mylinski?"

Dex stepped toward the doctor. "How is he? Will he live?"

Alyson stepped up next to Dex. She slipped her

palm in his and held on. Her skin was warm and soft, and Dex felt a surge of strength from her grip in spite of himself.

The doctor glanced from Dex to Alyson and back again. "Mr. Mylinski is in rough shape. He took three bullets to the chest. They seem to have missed vital organs, but he's lost a lot of blood. He made it through surgery, but I'm afraid we won't know anything more for a while."

"When can I talk to him?"

"I don't know how coherent he'll be."

"I need to talk to him. It's important." He pulled his wallet from his pocket and showed the doctor his D.A. shield and identification.

The doctor nodded. "All right." He turned and walked down the hall in the direction he had come.

Dex followed hard on the doctor's heels. Alyson fell into step beside him. They strode down the gleaming tile floor and entered the ICU.

A row of rooms set off by sliding-glass doors flanked each side of the long hall. In the center, nurses stood behind a long desk, eyes on machines monitoring patients in various stages of critical condition. The doctor slid open one of the doors and led them inside.

Al Mylinski was not a small man, but he looked small in the sea of white sheets. Tubes snaked from his arms, hooking him to an IV bag and various monitors. A clear oxygen tube threaded under his nose.

Dex opened and closed his fists by his sides. It seemed unreal to see Al Mylinski this way. Since Dex had first met him, he'd always been strong, able, with a crooked smile on his lips and a wry sense of humor twinkling in his eyes. A far cry from this shell of a man barely grasping life.

Alyson stepped close to the bed and laid her hand on Mylinski's, careful not to dislodge tubes. She stroked her fingers over the detective's skin. "Al."

Dex forced his feet to step up next to her. He bent over the still form. "Al? Can you hear me?"

Mylinski's eyes fluttered but remained closed.

"It's Dex. I need to talk to you."

His parched lips opened slightly. "Dex."

"What happened?"

"Got shot."

"I can see that. Did you see who shot you?"

"Asleep. Guess I should have worn Kevlar pajamas."

Dex couldn't help but smile. Here was the Mylinski he knew. Mere bullets couldn't diminish that sense of humor.

Mylinski opened his eyes for a second, then closed them again. "Hey, Alyson."

Tears sparkled in the corners of Alyson's eyes, but she didn't let them fall. "Hang in there, Al."

His face grimaced. "Trying."

"It was Smythe." Dex couldn't keep the snarl out of his voice when he pronounced the scum's name. "He called after he shot you. He found out you were looking for Connie Rasula."

Al tried to nod, the attempt ending in a painful grimace. "Did you find her? Did you talk to her?"

"She was dead. Raped and murdered on the deck outside her home."

"Smythe is covering his tracks."

"Any word on Jennifer Scott?"

"Found a large deposit in her bank account."

"So Smythe may have paid her to disappear."

"Don't think so."

"Why?"

"Wherever she went, she didn't take the money with her."

Dread gripped Dex's shoulders like a cold hand. After seeing firsthand the way Smythe had paid Connie Rasula for helping him, he didn't hold out much hope for Jennifer Scott. That is, if the scientist had actually helped Smythe. "Did you try to trace the money? Do we know if it came from Smythe?"

"Working on it. Don't know yet." Mylinski's eyes fluttered. He took a labored breath. "Even if it came from him, might not be able to prove it."

Alyson grasped Dex's arm, her touch gentle but firm. "He needs to rest."

Dex nodded. She was right. Mylinski needed all his strength to hang on to life. The detective couldn't help. Not until he recovered. And by then it might be too late. "One more thing, then I'll let you sleep."

"What?"

"I'm sorry I dragged you into this."

Mylinski tried to shake his head, the movement ending in a grimace. "You couldn't have kept me away." Jaw growing slack, he slipped back into a morphine sleep.

Dex stood at his bedside, listening to the beeps and whirs of monitors and watching Mylinski's chest rise and fall with each breath.

Alyson released Mylinski's fingers and placed her hand on Dex's arm, holding him, supporting him, the way she had since they'd watched the paramedics load the detective into the ambulance. In the waiting room he'd told her he didn't want her support. That he didn't need it. But standing here, feeling her touch, smelling her gentle scent so near, knowing she was beside him, seemed to fill a void inside him. A void he didn't know existed.

Or maybe he just hadn't wanted to acknowledge it.

She looked up at him, scanning his face. "Let's check on the results of that E.D.T.A. test. Jennifer might not have helped Smythe. Her disappearance might not have anything to do with him. And if she didn't help him, someone else did."

DEX STARED at the analysis Alyson handed him. Leaning on the edge of her desk in the DNA lab, he felt the now familiar sensation of his heart fluttering into double time as he looked at the piece of paper. "Insignificant amounts of E.D.T.A."

Alyson moved close and peered at the report. "The blood under Connie Rasula's fingernails was fresh."

"So if the money in Jennifer Scott's account came from Smythe, it wasn't to pay her for smuggling blood from the crime lab." He was relieved at the thought. He'd always thought the criminal justice system was run by the good guys—from beat cops to lab technicians to attorneys.

At least he'd believed that until he'd discovered Fitz's dirty secrets.

It felt good to know that in this case, the source of the blood under Connie Rasula's fingernails—the blood that had sprung Andrew Clarke Smythe from prison—wasn't an employee of the crime lab. He only hoped that didn't mean the corruption had come from another agency. His.

"Do you think the story she told Valerie about the Smythe Pharmaceuticals job could have been just that, a story?" Alyson asked.

He looked up from the paper, tension tightening the knot in his gut once again. "I don't like coincidences. Not where Smythe is concerned."

Alyson nodded. "Jennifer could have been involved with helping Smythe some other way. Some way that didn't entail smuggling blood from the crime lab.''

''Sounds possible. Any ideas?''

''She might have told him how to fake the rape.''

''I'm listening.''

''She used to volunteer for evidence collection.''

''Evidence collection? I thought she was a chemist.''

''Some of the people who work here volunteer to be on call to process crime scenes for jurisdictions that don't have their own crime scene units. I never used to because I always wanted to spend more time with you.''

He remembered those times. Times they'd spent working together on remodeling his house until late into the night. Times she'd appear at his office after he'd had a hard day in court and cajole him into enjoying dinner with her instead of just grabbing a sandwich from a vending machine. Times they spent all evening and night in bed with no thoughts of anything but each other. Dex shifted uncomfortably. ''So she could tell Smythe exactly how to stage a crime scene.''

''Or maybe she staged it herself.''

''I doubt it. There were a number of mistakes in the scene itself. Mistakes an experienced crime scene technician probably wouldn't make.''

Curiosity sparked in Alyson's eyes. "What kind of mistakes?"

"There was no evidence that Ms. Rasula was chloroformed, for one thing. Even though she insisted she was, her blood test came back clean. All of Smythe's assaults were blitz-style attacks. He sneaked up on his victim and covered her nose and mouth with chloroform."

"That's how he attacked me."

Anger surged through Dex's bloodstream at the thought of Smythe touching Alyson. He clenched his fingers tightly on the E.D.T.A. report and tried to stifle his rage. "And that's how Connie Rasula should have been attacked if the same perpetrator committed all the rapes. We should have seen evidence to back up her claims."

Alyson nodded. "I guess he didn't pay her enough."

"Or the person who set up the scene didn't know the importance of making the attack appear to be like the others."

"Which leaves Jennifer out."

"So it seems."

"She still could have told him how to do it. Or at least she could have given him the idea. That would be enough reason to offer her the job at Smythe Pharmaceuticals."

"And enough reason to make her disappear. Unfortunately the only way we can learn what her role was is to ask her.'' Silence hung between Dex and Alyson like a pall. As much as he didn't want to admit it, the chances of Jennifer Scott being alive were slim and growing slimmer.

"So we're back to his prison visitors. I was hoping not to have to face another scandal in the district attorney's office.'' The reference was out of his mouth before he could censor it. At one time he'd used allusions to her father to lash out at her, to pay her back for the choice she'd made—a choice that broke his heart. But now he wanted to bite back the words. Alyson had suffered enough. The last thing he wanted was to cause her more pain. He ran his fingers down her arm in an attempt to apologize for the blunder.

Alyson set her chin and met his eyes, as if determined not to let him see her flinch. "I can't believe John Cohen would do something like that, no matter how burned out and cynical he's become.''

Dex had to force himself not to nod in agreement. He couldn't believe it, either. But then, he hadn't been able to believe a lot of things over the years, and all of those things had come back to bite him. "John was the only one with access to Smythe in prison. He's the most likely candidate.''

"What about Smythe's defense attorney?''

Lee Runyon. Dex nodded slowly. He'd love to believe Runyon was Smythe's lackey. It would be much easier than coming to terms with the alternative: that his office was as corrupt as Neil Fitzroy's. And that once again reality had fallen far short of his perception.

Pushing himself up from the edge of Alyson's desk, he handed the test results back to her. "Maybe it's time we have a chat with Lee Runyon."

ALYSON HELD ON to her visor with one hand and the dash of the golf cart with the other. Dex sat beside her, piloting the cart through the twists and turns of the asphalt path. They'd tried to contact Runyon at his office downtown with no luck. He wasn't in. And he wasn't in court. That left only one place he could be. At a golf course.

It hadn't taken long to track him to University Ridge Golf Course on the far west side of town. The course was scenic, prestigious, and the tee fees were high. The logical place for a man like Runyon.

Alyson tried to shuck the tremor of nerves in her stomach. She didn't know Runyon well. Except for being cross-examined by him in court, she'd only seen him at a handful of her father's political functions. But what she knew of him hadn't endeared him to her. He struck her as a pompous man. One who liked to wear his wealth on his sleeve to make himself feel more important.

She spotted him right away on the seventh-hole green. The bright sunlight glared off his bald head as he lined up his putt. She pointed in his direction.

Dex swung the cart off the path. They bumped over the rough. Finally he came to a stop near the green and turned off the ignition. He turned to Alyson. "Well, here goes. Just follow my lead."

She nodded and climbed from the vehicle. She had no problem following Dex's lead. Especially where Runyon was concerned. The man reminded her of a bulldog—so homely he was cute until he sank those crooked teeth into your flesh. She'd felt those teeth more than once in the witness box while testifying about DNA evidence in a case. She didn't relish the thought of feeling his bite today. Not when she needed so much to find something, anything, that would lead them to Patrick. "I'm right behind you."

Dex strode across the grass and onto the green. His strides were even, his head held high. The picture of strength and confidence. A warrior who wouldn't be denied his victory.

Spirits buoying, she walked at his side. Runyon wouldn't know what hit him until it was too late.

With one smooth swing, Runyon sank his ball. When he stooped to scoop it out of the hole, his dark gaze landed on Dex and Alyson. "Well, what do we have here? I would think the district attorney's office and the crime lab would be too busy saving the world from big, bad criminals for the two of you to be out on the fairway this afternoon."

Dex shot him an all-business stare. "I need to have a word with you."

Runyon glanced at his golf partners. "Why don't you go on to the next hole? You could use the head start. I'm tired of standing around waiting."

With a bit of grumbling and a few insults tossed back at Runyon, the men gathered their clubs and sauntered on.

Runyon turned his hawklike eyes on Dex. "So, what is this about, Harrington? I sure hope it's not something that could have waited until I was back in the office tomorrow."

"When was the last time you talked to Andrew Smythe?"

"Ah. The Smythe pardon. I should have known that's what you'd want to talk about. I told you when we tried that case that you wouldn't win in the end. You really should have listened to me, you know."

Dex stared at him with a poker face. "When was the last time, Runyon?"

"I don't know. Ask my secretary. She does the billing."

"Did you know he's suspected of committing a rape and murder up in Minocqua?"

"No. But I'm sure if the cops up there had any solid evidence against Andy, I'd be up north right now seeing that his rights aren't trampled instead of enjoying this lovely June day on the course."

"Just wait," Alyson threatened. "The crime lab hasn't had time to complete the DNA testing."

Runyon shifted his eyes to her. "Would that be the same DNA testing that proved there is another man out there with identical DNA committing rapes while my client was behind bars?"

Alyson bit her tongue and glanced at Dex. She should have done as he said and let him do the talking. But something inside her wouldn't allow her to stand quietly by while her son—her life—was on the line. "That blood was planted, and you know it. My question is, how did you get Smythe's blood out of the prison without anyone noticing?"

Runyon quirked a brow and turned to Dex. "She has quite an imagination for a scientist."

Dex gave him a glare that would melt a more sensitive man. Or one with half a conscience. "I want to hear your answer."

"My answer? I've never taken anything from Andrew Clarke Smythe except my very reasonable and legitimate fees. And I never gave him anything except the best legal advice money could buy."

"Did you hire a private investigator for him?"

"What does it matter if I did? I hire private investigators to work on several of my clients' cases."

"And you act as a go-between?"

"Sometimes. What are you trying to get at here, Harrington?"

"I want to know how Andrew Clarke Smythe's blood found its way outside those prison walls."

"Have you ever considered that you may have the answer to that question already? That maybe Andy has a DNA double out there?"

"That's ridiculous and you know it." Alyson couldn't keep her mouth shut one second longer. "DNA is unique, just as people are unique. The only way Smythe could have a double is if he had an identical twin. And we all know he has no identical twin."

A slow grin spread across Runyon's face. "Do we?"

Doubt wound through Alyson's resolve like a grapevine through tree branches. She glanced at Dex.

A frown furrowed his brow. "He has no identical twin. I turned his life upside down preparing for his trial. I would have found a twin."

"To the best of my recollection," Runyon drawled, "Andy's parents refused to answer your questions."

Alyson remembered Dex's frustration in the months leading up to the trial. Not only had Smythe's parents refused to talk, but everyone within the influence of the Smythe money kept their mouths shut, as well. In the end, pure police work and scientific analysis had convicted the rapist.

Runyon hefted his golf bag to his shoulder.

"Well, none of that matters anyway. I doubt they'll be talking to you now, either. And I have to get to my golf game. Some of those boys I'm playing with are known for their cheating. I don't want to lose the hundred I have riding on this game because of a kicked ball."

"Not so fast." Dex held up a hand. "I have more questions for you."

"None that I'm going to answer. Haven't you heard of attorney-client privilege, counselor? I'm ethically bound to keep my client's confidences. And that includes the discussions I might or might not have had with a private investigator."

Alyson dug her fingernails into the palms of her hands. "You can't just walk away from this." Alyson's voice rang shrill in her ears. Desperate. "Smythe murdered a woman."

Runyon's eyebrows jutted toward his nonexistent hairline. "And I'll take that charge seriously only if you can show me evidence, Miz Fitzroy. Now I have eleven more holes to play. If you want to waste my time further, I trust you'll make an appointment at my office."

Alyson stared at his retreating back and tried to quell the tears of frustration surging for release. "Is it true, what he said? Can he stonewall us like that, no matter what he knows? Can he refuse to even give us the private investigator's name?"

"He can if he's not part of a conspiracy."

"In other words…"

"If he didn't do anything illegal to help Smythe break the law, he doesn't have to say a word. In fact, he'd probably be disbarred if he did."

"But if he staged a false rape to get Smythe pardoned?"

"He would be part of a conspiracy, and attorney-client privilege wouldn't apply."

Her heart soared with hope for a second, then crashed somewhere in the vicinity of her toes. "But unless he talks, we have no way to prove he's part of anything Smythe has done."

Dex turned toward the golf cart. "Correct. And that leaves only one thing for me to do."

"What's that?"

"It's time I have a talk with the governor. He won't want to hear about my resignation on the news tomorrow."

Chapter Eight

The door swung open and Dex strode into his office. He didn't say a word, merely offering Alyson a solemn glance before shrugging out of his suit jacket and sinking into his desk chair. Leaning back, he ran a hand over his face.

Alyson eyed him from the corner of the room. While he'd met with the governor, she'd waited in his office, since it was one of the few places they both agreed she'd be safe from Smythe. And though thoughts of her father's time between these four walls hovered in the back of her mind like a ghost, the problems of the past seemed insignificant compared to her worry for Patrick. And for Dex.

She was probably one of the few people on earth who knew exactly how much Dex's career meant to him. How he'd come from nothing, earning scholarships to get him through college and law school. How he'd worked night and day trying every case he could get his hands on, from the smallest misdemeanor until he worked his way up to felonies. And finally how he'd earned his way to an appointment from the governor and hopefully to election by the people in November. He'd put his heart and soul into this job. And looking at his face now, so pale and drawn, she knew exactly how much it cost him to give it up.

Standing, she set the paperback she'd been staring at on the chair seat, crossed the room and stopped next to his desk. "How are you holding up?"

He didn't glance at her, but stared straight ahead, eyes weary. "I'm fine."

"Right. You're downright peachy. Just like me." She hadn't meant to let sarcasm slip out, but she couldn't help it. It was so like Dex to withdraw into himself when facing a personal crisis. She'd seen him do it more than once. But he wasn't going to do it this time.

She stepped behind his chair and rested her hands on his shoulders as she'd done so many times before. His muscles were tense, bunching like coiled springs under his crisp white dress shirt. She dug her fingertips into the knots and began to knead.

He'd helped her so much these past days. If it wasn't for him—his shoulder to cry on, his strength to lean on, his determination to find Patrick—she didn't know how she would have survived. And now it was her turn to help him. And though she wasn't sure how to accomplish it, she'd give it her best shot. And the only place she knew to start was to get him talking. "How's the governor holding up?"

"He's not so fine."

"Not happy, eh?"

"To say the least."

"What reason did you give him for resigning?"

"The ever-vague 'personal reasons.'" The pain aching in his voice cut into her like a sharp blade.

She worried her bottom lip between her teeth. "There must be a way around this. Isn't there some way you can resign temporarily?"

He shook his head. "I don't know how Smythe found out about Mylinski's involvement in the case, but we can't take the chance that he'd sniff out a false resignation. There's too much at stake."

He was right. There was too much at stake. Far too much. And that left Dex only one option. He had to do as Smythe said.

Unless they could find Patrick before the press conference tomorrow.

Alyson continued to massage the knots out of his shoulder muscles, her mind racing with possibilities. "While you were with the governor, I was thinking about some things Runyon said."

Dex glanced over his shoulder and raised his eyebrows. "And?"

"What if Smythe's parents arranged for Connie Rasula to fake the rape? The Smythes certainly have enough money to make it worth Runyon's while to smuggle Andrew's blood out of prison.''

''I suppose it's possible. But the question is why?''

''What do you mean? Isn't it obvious? They're his parents.''

''That's not enough reason. Not for people like the Smythes. I doubt any one of them would risk one hair to save a family member. That family makes my background look positively wholesome.''

Alyson's hands stilled. Dex had mentioned before that he'd had a troubled family life growing up. But every time she'd pressed him to tell her more, he'd clammed up, as if unwilling to open himself that much. Or unwilling to relive the memories. ''Do you want to talk about it?''

''Seems Andrew's father beat his mother and his mother passed the abuse on to Andrew. Among other lovely things.''

''I didn't mean Andrew Smythe's family. I meant yours.''

Dex stilled. He didn't look at her, but she didn't need to see his face to know how his jaw clenched and his eyes narrowed guardedly behind his wire-rimmed glasses. Tension pulsed off him in waves. ''Some things are better left alone.''

''And some things are better if you talk about them.''

He shook his head, the office light sparking off

his blond hair. "This isn't one of them. Trust me. We both have enough pain to deal with in the present. We don't need to go looking for more." He stood from his chair, effectively shucking her hands from his shoulders. But instead of pacing to the far corner of the room, he planted his feet, as if something was keeping him rooted to the spot.

She searched for words to say—words that would convince him to open himself to her. But none formed on her lips. She raised a hand, letting it hover near his arm. She wanted to touch him again, to reach him, but she didn't know how.

She'd never known how.

She let her hand fall to her side. "You don't think talking to Smythe's parents would do any good?"

"I didn't say that. Right now I think we need to explore every possibility. We have no other choice." He stepped away from the desk, away from her.

Standing alone, she placed her hands on the back of the chair. She'd been foolish to think she could help him. Or that he would accept her help. He was the same man, after all. The man who'd survived who-knew-what horrors in childhood. The man who'd leveraged his way into the district attorney's office with nothing but hard work and stubbornness.

The man who'd walked away from her the moment she'd failed to live up to his impossible standards.

Nothing she could do would make him change. Not a year and a half ago. And not now. The only thing she could do was worry about herself. Because she faced more dangers than Andrew Clarke Smythe posed. She'd given Dex her heart once, and it had almost destroyed her. She couldn't let herself fall into that trap again.

DEX SLAMMED the car door and looked up at the looming Gothic Tudor-style mansion that the Smythe family called home when they were in Madison. Sheer stone walls stretched in long wings on either side of the entry, gray as weathered bone. Sharp-angled roofs stabbed into the cloud-darkened sky like spears raised in battle. Windows stared down at Alyson and him like cold eyes.

He glanced at the half dozen cars parked in the circle drive and then at Alyson as she climbed from the car. "Judging from the cars, someone's entertaining."

Alyson followed his gaze. "Richard or Patrice?"

"Must be Patrice. I had Maggie place a call to Smythe Pharmaceuticals earlier today. Richard's out of town."

"Is that good or bad?"

He shrugged and circled the car. "Doesn't matter. Both are equally hard to deal with."

Alyson nodded and looked up at the house. She was walking into a lion's den and she didn't even seem to know it. Or maybe she did. He doubted it would make a difference. She would clearly do anything to get Patrick back, whatever the cost. He'd bet she was a wonderful mother, so loving and giving. Always concerned about others' needs.

Just as she'd been concerned about him when he'd returned from his trip to talk to the governor. He pressed his lips into a grim line. He'd never told anyone about his family, but he'd come close to spilling it all to Alyson.

Thank God she'd let the subject drop. Reliving the past didn't do any good. It would only have served to remind him of his vulnerability during a time when he especially couldn't afford to be vulnerable. Or weak. He focused his attention on the mansion. "Are you ready?"

Alyson shivered and started to climb the stairs leading to the house. She ripped her attention from the windows and met his gaze. "Just nervous, that's all. I keep thinking that Andrew Smythe could be up there, looking down on us."

"If he is, he has more to be nervous about than you do. I'd love to get my hands around the bastard's neck. Unfortunately the best we can hope for is to find out if his parents helped him get out of prison. Or have any idea who did."

"Or if they're helping him hide Patrick."

"Knowing Patrice Smythe, I don't see that happening. But that doesn't mean she won't be able to

clue us in about who might be helping him. The
trick will be getting her to talk.''

Alyson gave an eager nod and quickened her pace
up the stone staircase.

Dex lengthened his stride to keep up. ''Don't get
your hopes up. Like Runyon pointed out, they both
refused to talk to me two years ago. There's no reason to assume Patrice will talk to me now.''

''She has to. I can't bear to think of Patrick
spending another night away from me.'' Setting her
chin, Alyson focused on the grand entry. ''We've
got to find him.''

''And we will. I promise you. We will.'' Reaching the door, Dex pressed the doorbell. Chimes echoed through stone. Before the ringing stopped, the
door opened and a small woman who resembled a
delicate bird stood in front of them. ''May I help
you?''

Dex remembered the petite housekeeper from the
months leading up to Smythe's trial. She'd always
met him at the door. And she'd always turned him
away with instructions to talk to the Smythes' attorney. He gritted his teeth. Only the filthy rich
could duck talking to law enforcement. But this time
he wouldn't take no for an answer. If she tried that
tack again, he'd bull his way through the door and
force them to talk with his bare hands, if need be.

''Is Mr. or Mrs. Smythe in?'' Dex asked.

The woman nodded. "Mrs. Smythe is in, but she's busy with guests."

"Tell her Dex Harrington is here to see her. Tell her I need to talk to her about her son."

"I'm sorry. She really is busy."

"Tell her I'm here to apologize."

He could feel Alyson's eyebrows raise at the obvious lie. The housekeeper didn't seem to notice. She merely nodded and pulled the door open wide.

They stepped into the grand entry hall. Dex looked around the foyer, taking in the way the crystal chandelier threw droplets of light on the oak floors and art-covered walls. Stairs swept up to the level above with the drama of a Southern plantation house. Amazing how some people lived. Coming from his poor background, he might be envious if he didn't know the seedy side of the Smythes' seemingly perfect lives.

The housekeeper gestured to an arched doorway. "Have a seat in the living room. I'll tell Mrs. Smythe you're here."

They stepped into a living room furnished in cream and gold and lowered themselves into plush chairs. Dex hated sitting still like this, as if waiting for something bad to happen. He itched to pace the length of the room. Instead he followed Alyson's example and took in the scenery, glancing out one of the plate-glass panes facing the lake. The capitol dome rose out of the fog on the opposite shore.

"It's about time you apologized, Mr. Harrington. After all you did to my son, it's surprising you have the guts to show your face here."

Dex turned in his chair and looked into the face of Patrice Smythe. Whereas the housekeeper had always reminded him of a delicate sparrow, Mrs. Smythe resembled a bird of prey. Sharp eyes riveted on Dex. Rouged cheeks hollowed below high cheekbones. And her lips pressed into a severe line. She hadn't changed in the past two years. If anything she'd grown harder.

Dex tried to assume an appropriately chagrined expression. "I just need to clear a couple things up first, if you don't mind."

"I have guests, so make it quick."

"When is the last time you saw your son, Mrs. Smythe?"

"The afternoon he was pardoned. I planned a party for him. He stayed five minutes. Why?"

"Did you visit him while he was in prison?"

"Me? Go to that awful place?"

"How did you communicate with your son?"

"Through his attorney, Mr. Runyon."

"And did you pay Mr. Runyon to act as a go-between?"

She narrowed her mascara-rimmed eyes. "This doesn't sound like an apology."

Anger churned in his gut. He couldn't hold it in any longer. Just the thought of apologizing for taking Andrew Clarke Smythe off the streets made him want to hit something. "Your son was guilty of victimizing six women. I have nothing to apologize for."

"You've read the papers, haven't you, Mr. Harrington? My son didn't rape those women. Someone else is out there. Why don't you focus on finding him instead of on embarrassing our family? Now if you aren't going to apologize, I have nothing more to say to you. Mary Ann will show you out."

Alyson jumped up from her chair before Patrice Smythe had the chance to turn around. "Wait." Chin raised in determination, she looked as if she was ready to take on an army to get to the truth.

Patrice looked down on her as if she were a dirty spot in the carpet.

"We didn't come to talk about your son's past, Mrs. Smythe."

Patrice arched plucked eyebrows. "Why did you come?"

"Do you know if your son has a baby?"

"A baby? Andrew?"

"Yes."

"And why are you asking me?"

"You're his mother. I just thought—"

"If he has a baby, he hasn't told me. Not that he would share that kind of news with his mother. Who's the mother of this baby?"

"Me."

Her gaze darkened. "Are you accusing Andrew of something? Or are you here to see what kind of payoff you can get?"

Just the suggestion that Andrew Smythe was Patrick's father made Dex want to set the record straight. He caught Alyson's pleading glance and shut his mouth. He'd struck out when it came to handling Patrice Smythe. The only option left was to let Alyson take a shot. He clenched his hands and said nothing.

Alyson looked back at Patrice and splayed her hands, palms up, in front of her. "I just want my baby back. I want to know he's okay."

"That's a likely story."

"It's true, Mrs. Smythe. Please."

"Well, if it's money you want, you've come to the wrong person. You'd be better off going to his father. God knows he's paid off enough of his own whores over the years. I suppose he'll write you a nice check, too." She looked back at Dex. "I don't know what you're up to, bringing her here, but I'm not going to stand for it. I want you both out of my house. Now." She whirled around and strode away.

Alyson's shoulders slumped.

Dex stood from his chair. He'd warned her not to get her hopes up, but she obviously had. "Patrice Smythe was a long shot. We did our best."

She shook her head. "I hoped that as a woman and mother, she'd understand. I never dreamed she'd think I was trying to extort money by claiming Patrick was Andrew Smythe's son.''

"You tried."

"I can imagine how it made you feel. I'm sorry."

He waved aside her concern. He couldn't accept any more concern from her today. Each tender word from her mouth made him want to gather her in his arms, to claim her lips, to never let her go.

"Please follow me." The meek voice of the birdlike housekeeper penetrated his thoughts.

Holding out a hand, he helped Alyson from her chair and they followed the woman across the plush carpet into the marble-floored foyer.

The housekeeper reached the door and opened it, standing to the side to let them exit. As Alyson stepped past her, the woman whispered, "Mrs. Smythe wouldn't know about any baby. Andrew doesn't confide in his mother."

Adrenaline jolted through Dex's bloodstream.

Alyson grabbed the woman's arm. "Who does he confide in? You?"

She shook her birdlike head. "Not me. His sister."

Dex stepped up close behind. "His sister? He doesn't have a sister."

"Half sister. The daughter of one of those whores Mrs. Smythe likes to talk about." An edge of bitterness crept into the woman's voice. She glanced down the hall as if to be sure her employer hadn't crept back within hearing range. The long hall was empty and women's voices drifted from one of the rooms.

Dex's mind raced. He scrutinized the woman's face. "How do you know all this?"

"Because my mother is that whore. Though my sister and I have different fathers."

Dex searched her face. "Who is your half sister?"

The woman's forehead furrowed. "Her name is Maggie Daugherty."

Chapter Nine

Dex grabbed Alyson's arm and led her from the Smythe mansion. The clouds had opened up while they were inside and rain pelted his face. The echo of the door slamming behind them clashed with the rumble of thunder.

"Maggie Daugherty?" Alyson said in a tone of disbelief. "As in the same Maggie Daugherty who works in your office?"

"One and the same." Dex's voice came out in a monotone that belied the turmoil inside him. He looked over his shoulder at the Smythe house. A silhouette darkened an upstairs window. Mrs. Smythe? The housekeeper? Or Andrew himself? "Let's get out of here."

Alyson nodded and scampered for the car.

Once inside his sedan and on the road, Dex let the shock of the housekeeper's statement filter through his mind.

"I just can't believe it," Alyson said, voicing his

thoughts. ''Maggie has been looking at me strangely lately, but I assumed it was because of what my father did. It never occurred to me that she might have something to do with Smythe.''

Dex's thoughts had been following the same lines. Should he have seen a resemblance? Should he have noticed if she seemed more interested in Andrew's case than the others that coursed through the office? ''If I remember correctly, Maggie was hired right after I started work on Smythe's rape case.''

''She took the job to influence the case.''

''Or to feed Runyon any information she could get her hands on.''

''It didn't seem to help Smythe's case. You convicted him anyway.''

''Yeah. But maybe it helped her come up with a plan for getting him out.''

''Do you think she's the one who helped Smythe smuggle his blood out of prison?''

''It's possible.''

''But she would have been on the prison sign-in sheet if she'd gone to see him. Of course she could have had help. Runyon?''

''Or John Cohen.'' He hated to admit that one of the A.D.A.s he'd worked with for years was the better suspect, but until a few minutes ago he'd no idea the office receptionist had a connection to Andrew Clarke Smythe. He couldn't afford to hide his head in the sand any longer. "They work in the same office. They are in contact every day."

Alyson's face fell. "If Maggie visited Runyon's office, it might make people suspicious, but no one would think twice if she popped in to talk with Cohen."

"Exactly."

"So what do we do next?"

"We have a chat with Maggie and find out if the Smythe's housekeeper is telling the truth."

"And if the housekeeper is right...if Maggie is Andrew Smythe's sister and the one person he confides in—" She stopped as if afraid to go on.

Dex finished for her. "Then maybe she's also the one person he would trust to take care of a kidnapped baby."

ALYSON FOLLOWED DEX up the combination of stairs and patios snaking around the outside of the condominium his office employment records had shown was Maggie Daugherty's address. By the time they'd finished their meeting with Patrice Smythe, Maggie had long since left the office. It was just as well. This way they would get a chance to take a peek inside her home. Babies didn't travel light. If Maggie was housing a baby in the conservative condo, there would be telltale signs. Bottles and baby food jars littering the kitchen counters. The scent of diapers. Or even a coo or a cry. If Patrick was here, they would know it.

Pressure bore down on Alyson's lungs like the damp rain, making it hard to breathe. Every nerve pressed her to race up those stairs, break open the door and gather her baby into her arms. Biting her lower lip, she forced herself to take the condo stairs at an even pace.

When they reached the front door, Dex turned to look at her. "We need to play this cool. Just follow my lead."

Alyson nodded and took what she hoped would be a calming breath. Dex knew Maggie better than she did. She was glad he was there with her, taking the lead. Left to her own devices, she would probably just push her way inside and ransack the place until she found her son. She held her breath as Dex pressed the buzzer.

Footsteps sounded from inside the house. A dead bolt slid back. The door inched open and one of Maggie's brown eyes peered out through the crack. "Dex?"

"I need a word with you, Maggie. It's important."

The door swung open. When Maggie spotted Alyson in the shadows behind Dex, her eyes narrowed.

Dex stepped forward. "May we come in?"

Maggie looked from Alyson to Dex. "I'm in the

middle of making dinner. Can't this wait until tomorrow?''

''I'm sorry, but it can't. I have to talk to you
tonight. You see, I think there's a problem in the
office.''

Maggie's eyes rounded, but instead of conveying
surprise, she looked as if she was bracing herself for
an accusation. ''Problem? What kind of problem?''

''Could we talk about it inside? It's rather wet out
here and the news isn't something I want to share
with your neighbors.''

''All right.'' Maggie closed the door and unfastened the security chain. When she opened the door,
her face was a perfectly composed mask. ''Come
in.''

Dex and Alyson stepped inside, and Maggie shep-
herded them into a small formal living room off the
foyer. ''Please sit down.''

Alyson perched on the edge of a chair, but Dex
remained standing.

So did Maggie. ''Now what is this problem, Dex?
And how can I help?''

Alyson's ears hummed. Maggie could help by
giving Patrick back. She could help by helping them
put her brother back in prison where he belonged.
And where—if she *had* helped her brother—she belonged, as well. Alyson clenched her hands in her
lap. She had to keep her cool if she was going to

find Patrick. She combed the room casually with her gaze, but no baby paraphernalia caught her notice.

Dex, too, looked around the room then focused on Maggie. "I think John Cohen is taking bribes."

"John Cohen?" Maggie echoed, but she didn't seem surprised. "What makes you think that?"

"It's in relation to the Andrew Clarke Smythe case."

Other than a blink, Maggie showed no outward signs that the name meant anything special to her. "He's the rapist the governor pardoned, right?"

"Right. We think Cohen helped Smythe smuggle blood out of prison, then planted it under the fingernails of a staged rape victim."

Maggie's gaze shifted to Alyson. "Is that why she's here? Because she performed DNA tests on that blood?"

"Yes. Alyson has been helping me with the scientific aspects of the case. We also believe Jennifer Scott, a forensic chemist at the State Crime Lab, may be involved."

Maggie nodded, seemingly buying his explanation. "So what do you want me to do? I don't know anything about what Cohen does in his free time." If Alyson wasn't mistaken, the edge of defensiveness was creeping into Maggie's voice. She glanced at Dex. If he caught it, he gave no sign.

"I want you to help me set Cohen up. If he's involved in helping Smythe, I want evidence."

"Why me?"

"Because I don't know how far the corruption reaches in the office. I don't know if I can trust any of the other assistant district attorneys."

Alyson glanced out the door and into the foyer. She couldn't sit in this living room another second. She had to find a way to look around the rest of the house. "Excuse me, Maggie. But could I use your rest room?"

Maggie's face drained of color. "I'd rather you didn't. I've been having problems with the plumbing lately."

"Oh, I just need to blow my nose. I won't tax the plumbing."

Maggie's glance flew around the room as if she was searching for a way out. "I'll go get you a box of tissues."

Alyson sprang to her feet. "Don't bother. You're busy with Dex. I can find the bathroom myself. I'll only be a minute." She strode for the living room door.

Maggie stepped in front of her. "Really, it's no bother. Why don't you take a seat. I'll be—"

Dex stepped forward. Reaching out, he grasped Maggie's arm. "I need you to approach Cohen with a false deal, Maggie. An undercover detective will pose as a defense lawyer looking to broker a deal for his incarcerated client."

Seeing her chance, Alyson ducked out the archway and half ran down the hall. She ducked into the kitchen and attached family room first. Grey countertops rimmed the perimeter of the small room, clean and neat. No signs of bottles or baby food. Crossing the floor, Alyson wrenched open the refrigerator door. Wine, cheese and plain yogurt stared back at her. No formula. No baby food. Her heart fell.

Stepping around the long counter that served as a breakfast bar, she searched the family room with her gaze. A few magazines and a smattering of romance novels cluttered the coffee table. But no baby swing or pacifier or any sign Maggie had even thought of housing a baby caught Alyson's eye.

She darted back into the hallway. There were only three more rooms to search. The bathroom and two closed doors. Her heart hammered in her ears, all but drowning out the sound of Dex's voice, outlining detail after detail of the false plot to get John Cohen to incriminate himself.

She scurried down the hall to the first closed door. Opening it, she slipped inside. Rain and approaching night made the room dim. But Alyson could make out a queen-size bed with a floral spread and an assortment of women's clothes draped over one end, as if someone had discarded them while searching for something to wear. Maggie's bedroom, no doubt. After a quick perusal, Alyson ducked back into the hallway. A quick glance in the bathroom yielded nothing.

Maggie's protests rose from the living room.

Alyson was running out of time. Sooner or later Dex would run out of false plans, and Maggie would come looking for her. She had to get a peek inside that last closed door before that happened.

She scampered down the hallway, closed her hand over the cool brass knob and turned. The knob held. It was locked. Elation shuddered through Alyson, chased by panic. Maggie was hiding something, all right. And it was behind this locked door. Alyson had to figure out a way to get inside. She wouldn't leave—she couldn't leave—until she got a look inside that room. And a simple privacy lock wasn't about to keep her out.

Bending, she peered at the knob. Sure enough, in the center was a small hole. Just like the knobs in her own house.

She crept back down the hall to the kitchen. She crossed to the desk and glanced through the unpaid bills and correspondence until she found a small container of paper clips. She'd locked herself out of the bedrooms in her house once before. And that's when she'd discovered the true value of paper clips.

Grabbing a clip from the box, she bent the curved wire straight and returned to the locked door. Hands shaking, she slipped the wire into the hole and poked for the mechanism. Silence came from the living room. Either Dex had run out of things to say, or he was wrestling Maggie to the ground to keep her from racing down the hall.

Alyson's heart beat in her ears like heavy rain on a tin roof. She poked and prodded with the wire. Finally it slipped into the mechanism. She gave the knob a turn and pushed inside the room.

With draperies drawn, this room was even darker than Maggie's bedroom. Alyson searched the darkness, willing her eyes to adjust. A bed hulked in one corner, along with a neat pile of large boxes. Or was that a crib? A crib holding her sweet baby? She held her breath and reached for the light switch.

A hand closed around her wrist and another around her throat. "Hello, Alyson. Did you miss me?"

Chapter Ten

A strangled scream split the air.

Alyson.

Dex's heart slammed against his rib cage. Releasing Maggie's arm, he raced for the hall. There could be only one reason for that scream, and it had nothing to do with Alyson finding the baby.

Smythe was here.

Reaching under his jacket, he withdrew the .38 nestled in his shoulder holster. He hadn't told Alyson he had a gun. He knew how she felt about them, and he didn't want to worry her. But he was glad he had it now.

A door on the far end of the hall stood ajar. Dex raced toward it. Gun poised, he kicked the door wide and swept the room with his gaze.

Alyson lay on the floor amid some boxes, holding her hand to her head. A window gaped open behind her. She raised her green eyes to Dex. Bright red blood mingled with the auburn of her hair and stained her fingers. "He's gone. Through the window."

Making another sweep of the room to be sure, Dex glanced out the open window. A manicured lawn stretched only a few feet below. An easy getaway. Somewhere in the distance, a car engine purred to life. Dex fell to his knees beside Alyson.

"Find Smythe. He's getting away." She tried to push him to his feet, her hands leaving bloodstains on his jacket and shirt. "I'm okay. Really."

"You're not okay, and Smythe is long gone."

Alyson sagged against him. Blood trickled down her forearm in a tiny rivulet. Blood and strands of her hair clung to the sharp edge of a glass-and-steel coffee table nearby.

Maggie's shadow stretched into the room in the light streaming from the doorway. "What happened? What was she doing in here? This is just a storeroom. I thought she said she had to use the rest room."

"You know damn well what happened. Your brother slammed Alyson's head into that table."

"My brother?"

"We know Andrew Smythe is your half brother, Maggie."

The woman's face blanched even whiter than before.

Dex didn't bother explaining. "Call 9-1-1. Tell

them to send an ambulance and the police. And make it fast.''

Alyson gripped his arm. "No police. No ambulance. I'm fine. Really.''

"You're hurt. You're bleeding all over.''

"It's nothing. Cuts to the head always bleed a lot. We can't call the police. He said—''

"You need medical attention. Smythe be damned.''

"You can drive me to the hospital.''

Her green eyes seemed unnaturally dark, even in the dim light of the room. Probably a concussion. He had to get her to a hospital. And he had to get her there now. "Fine. Put your arms around my neck. Can you do that?''

She did as he said.

He lifted her to her feet. "Can you stand?''

She did, leaning against him for balance. Wadding up a wash cloth he found in an open storage box, he pressed it to the cut on her scalp. "Hold this tight." Looping his free arm around her, he helped her walk from the room, still holding his gun in the other hand. Maggie didn't seem dangerous, but he wasn't taking any chances.

Maggie moved out of the way and let them pass. "She had no right snooping in my house. And she had no right scaring Andrew that way. He's a free man, like any other free man. He has the right to visit my house without being harassed.''

Dex shot her a look he hoped drilled into her misguided soul. ''As far as I'm concerned, Andrew Clarke Smythe doesn't have the right to take another breath. Tell him that for me, would you?''

DEX SMOOTHED CLEAN SHEETS on the bed in his guest bedroom and listened to sounds filtering through the door of the adjoining bathroom. The doctor at the Meriter Hospital emergency room had stitched up the cut in Alyson's scalp and had diagnosed her with a slight concussion. Dex would have felt better if she'd stayed in the hospital overnight for observation, but she wouldn't hear of it. Finally he'd agreed to take her home to his guest room. He'd bed down in the empty adjacent room. The master bedroom on the first level was too far away after what she'd just gone through. At least this way he could stay close enough to keep an eye on her, yet not be forced to sleep in the same room. He didn't need to tempt himself. Being one bedroom away was bad enough.

He fluffed the pillows and threw them into place at the head of the bed.

A pulsing whir filtered through the adjoining bathroom door. Alyson's breast pump. He'd heard it before in the time she'd been staying with him and each time he'd had trouble shutting the images from his mind. Images of the device fitting over her breasts, pulling at her nipples. The way he used to with his mouth. The way he wanted to again.

He grasped the television remote. He couldn't stand here and let himself remember. The good memories would only tempt him. And the bad memories hurt too damn much. He switched on the set.

The ten o'clock news snapped on the screen. Dex stared at the blond anchorwoman and forced himself to listen to her words and to keep his mind off Alyson.

A losing battle.

"Sources in the governor's office have confirmed that interim District Attorney Dexter Harrington will resign from his position."

Dex's heart stilled, then launched into double time. "Damn."

"We were unable to reach Mr. Harrington for comment, but the same sources stated that the district attorney decided to resign after the governor's recent pardon of convicted sex offender Andrew Clarke Smythe. Harrington will reportedly take full responsibility for the mistaken conviction at a press conference tomorrow."

The bathroom door opened and Alyson stepped out. She was dressed in the oversize Wisconsin Badger T-shirt he'd given her, the hem reaching to the middle of her thighs. Unnaturally pale, she gripped the door jamb for support. Her concerned expression made it clear she'd heard the broadcast. "They made it sound like Smythe is innocent."

"Yes. And that I railroaded him." The muscles in his shoulders knotted. "When I was at the governor's office, I never mentioned anything about the Smythe case. There's no way one of the governor's people leaked that story. The whole thing reeks of Smythe."

"And when you add the apologies Smythe insisted you make, it's going to look like the sources were right."

A weight settled on Dex's shoulders. Smythe had promised he'd destroy him. He hadn't been kidding. "First Patrick, then my career, and now my reputation. What do I have left?" He looked at Alyson, at the concern in her eyes, the pallor of her face. Smythe wouldn't get near her. Not again. Dex would make sure of it if he had to kill the bastard himself.

He stared out the window at the rain glistening on the roof mixing with the sheen of the lake stories below the window. "I feel so out of control. Like Smythe can do anything he wants to me, and I don't have anything to say about it."

She reached out and laid a hand on his arm, stilling him in his tracks. "I feel the same way."

Dex looked down at her. Her face was as pale as the bandage around her head. "Oh, hell, I'm sorry."

"About what?"

"I'm going on about lack of control of my career when you've lost so much more. A child."

"Our child."

"Yes. Our child." He stepped to where she gripped the door jamb and placed his hand over her fingers. Her skin was soft to his touch, her fingers fine and long. Just the way her hand had always felt in his.

"I know how much your career means to you, Dex. You don't have to explain or justify or apologize for your feelings."

Her words penetrated his defenses and hit bone. Once again she had seen through him, reached out to him, and said the right thing. Just the thing he needed to hear. He searched her face. For what, he didn't know. And she returned his gaze. Open. Vulnerable.

He swallowed into a dry throat. "You look like you're going to fall over. The least I can do is get you into bed."

Her glance rested on the bed before he realized what he'd said.

She released the door jamb and crossed the distance to the bed. She sat back against the headboard and stretched her long legs in front of her. The white bandage at her hairline stood out against her auburn hair. She looked swamped in his oversize T-shirt. Slender, delicate and in need of protection. She'd been through so much. With her father, with him, and now at the hands of Smythe. Yet when he needed her, she was there for him with a reassuring word. A touch. A firm grasp on reality. Under that delicate shell beat a heart stronger than steel.

A heart he knew was breaking with each day that passed.

He stepped to the side of the bed, wanting to touch her, to reassure her. "We won't give up."

She nodded, flinching slightly with the movement.

"And we'll find Patrick."

"I know." She reached out and took his hand in hers. "Thank you, Dex."

"For what?"

"For being beside me. For going through this with me. I don't know how I ever could have survived this alone."

He didn't know how she'd survived all she had alone. Learning she was pregnant, giving birth, waking in the middle of the night to the baby's cries. "Does it scare you sometimes? Having that little life totally dependent on you?"

"Are you kidding? It petrifies me."

"How do you deal with it?"

"I concentrate on the love. I let the rest fall away and concentrate on the love."

Could he do that? Could he concentrate on the love? His mother had been loving. Surely he had that in him somewhere. And God knew, Alyson provided a good example.

She watched him, her emerald eyes scrutinizing, assessing. Her hair spread like a silken auburn pool over the white cotton pillowcases. Her skin was nearly as white as the bandage capping her head.

He glanced at the sheet and comforter folded back at the foot of the bed. He should raise the sheet, cover her long, smooth legs and walk out the door, but somehow he couldn't make his hands obey.

A slight smile curved the corners of her lips. "You worry, don't you? About being a father?"

The weight bore down on him. "Shouldn't I worry? I don't have much of a role model."

A little crease formed between her eyebrows. She pursed her lips as if deep in thought. "You've never told me about your father. Not in all the time we were together."

"He wasn't a man to be proud of."

"But he was your father."

"He was a drunk." Memories of his father rushed through his mind in a tumultuous river. He tried to block them, to dam them up as he had for years, but he couldn't.

Alyson didn't say a word, she merely watched him as if waiting for him to go on.

"He had several run-ins with the law, including petty theft and a hefty number of DUI arrests. He also should have been brought up on domestic abuse charges a couple of times, but he sweet-talked my mom out of reporting him.''

''He hit your mother?''

He nodded. ''And occasionally me. Always when he was drunk. The booze was always his excuse, but really he was just a pathetic loser.''

''I'm sorry, Dex. I didn't know.''

''I didn't want you to. I didn't want anyone to.'' And he still didn't. But looking into her eyes, so compassionate and accepting, he couldn't do anything but tell her whatever she wanted to know.

''So he must have done jail time.''

''Not enough. Not nearly enough. He was a charming man. He sweet-talked the judge, my mother, me. That man was forgiven more sins than most people ever commit.''

''So what happened to him?''

''He's on parole. In a halfway house here in Madison.''

Her eyebrows arched toward the bandage at her hairline. ''He's still alive?''

''Yes. Though he doesn't deserve to be.''

''You talk about him as if he were dead.''

''I like to think of him that way. It makes things easier. And more just.''

''Things? What things?''

''My mother's death.''

She leaned toward him, as if trying to see into his

mind, to understand what he was saying. The crease between her eyebrows deepened. "How would that help?"

"Easy. The bastard killed her."

Chapter Eleven

Alyson's eyes widened and a gasp escaped her lips. "How did it happen?"

Pain throbbed through the muscles in Dex's neck and shoulders. He didn't want to talk about it. He didn't want to remember. One minute he'd been hiding his head in the sand, telling himself that his father would someday quit drinking, someday stay on the right side of the law, someday become a real father and husband. And the next thing he knew, he'd lost everything. His mother, his home and the bastard he'd pinned so many hopes on. "He was driving drunk and hit a tree. Nothing new. The only difference was, my mother was in the car. She was killed on impact. He walked into a prison cell."

"How old were you when it happened?"

"High school. Barely fourteen. I lived in a succession of foster homes until I became of age." He blew a stream of air through tight lips. "So that's why I don't talk about the bastard. He never cared about my mother or me, no matter how we both wanted to pretend he did. Booze was the only thing he cared about.'' Dex rolled his shoulders, trying to relieve the pressure, the pain. ''When he was done serving time for Mom's death, he went right back to drinking and driving and stealing to finance his bar tab. He's lived in jails, prisons and halfway houses ever since.''

Alyson's fingers closed tightly around his. ''I'm so sorry, Dex. I'm so very sorry.'' Compassion ached in her voice. Compassion and sympathy and caring. But no pity. And for that he was profoundly grateful.

He looked deep into her emerald eyes. He'd loved her once. So much it had frightened him. And looking at her now, he could almost believe his love had never really died. That it was still there, strong as ever. Tempting him to trust. To forgive. To take her in his arms and promise her she would never be alone again.

And that he would never be alone.

Closing his eyes, he slipped his hand from hers and turned away. He had to get out of this room. He had to think. He opened his eyes and strode for the door. ''I'll be back in the night to check your pupils.''

''Dex?''

He stopped, but didn't face her. He couldn't. If he looked into her eyes once more, he might just lose all sense of reality. He might just let himself fall back into her arms. Fall back into his dreams. ''Yes?''

''You'll make a great dad. Trust me. You're nothing like your father. There's more love inside you than you'll ever know.''

Dex stepped out of the room and closed the door behind him. He wanted to trust her. Not just about being a good father to Patrick. He wanted to trust her with his heart, his soul. And that scared him more than Andrew Clarke Smythe ever could.

ALYSON STARED at the closed door long after Dex left. His words echoed in her ears. His pain ached in her heart.

Her father had been greedy, corrupt and unconscionable. But that part of him hadn't surfaced until she was an adult, more able to deal with his betrayal. Dex's awakening to his father's sins had come much earlier. And the fact that his father had killed his mother made it all the more impossible to accept.

She sank into the pillows and switched off the bedside lamp. It all made sense to her now. The feeling she always got that if she crossed the line, he would write her off. And the fact that he had done exactly that when she'd hesitated to believe his accusation against her father.

She tried to close her eyes, tried to sleep. But

despite her throbbing head and weary bones, blessed unconsciousness wouldn't come.

She couldn't help thinking of Dex in the next room, alone with his bitter memories. If only she could have held him in her arms, kissed him until the shadows disappeared from his eyes.

She shook her head. He would never have accepted her touch, her tenderness. Even if she could have given it.

She'd loved Dex with her whole heart, her whole being. When he'd turned her away, it had almost killed her. And in the last fifteen months, nothing had changed. She still loved him, still yearned for his touch, his companionship, the glow in his eyes that once was there when he looked at her.

But now she knew why Dex could never give himself fully. Why she'd always felt as if she were walking a tightrope when they were together. Why he'd been so quick to write her off when she'd taken her first misstep. "Maybe it wasn't me who was afraid to trust, Dex. Maybe it was you all along."

SMOKE.

Dex jolted awake. His heart rattled against his ribs. He couldn't see. He couldn't breathe. He fumbled for the light he'd set next to him on the floor of the empty room. Finding the switch, he flicked it on. Nothing but darkness met his gaze.

He threw the blanket aside and scrambled to his

feet. He didn't need a light to confirm what he already knew. The room was filled with smoke. There was a fire in the house.

Alyson.

Pulling on his pants and shirt, he crossed the room in three steps and touched the door with an open hand. The wood was cool to the touch. Good. The fire wasn't right outside his door. But he had to hurry. Smoke could kill long before fire ever showed its flame.

The smoke was stronger in the hallway, thicker. He crouched low, trying to find clearer air closer to the floor. There was a full-blown fire, all right. He could hear the crackle of flame over the pounding of his pulse. He wasn't sure how far up the stairs it reached, but one thing was clear: they had to get out of here.

Groping his way the few steps down the dark hall, he located the door to the guest room and pushed it open. He ducked inside and shut it behind him. Through the haze and darkness, he could make out Alyson's form on the bed. "Alyson. Wake up. There's a fire."

She stirred, then jolted into a sitting position. Her hair tangled around her face. Her eyes shone bright in the moonlight filtering through the window. "Fire?"

"Hurry." He grabbed her hand and half lifted her out of the bed. They wouldn't be able to escape by the staircase, that was for certain. The hall was already choked with smoke, much of it pouring under the bedroom door with each second that passed. They'd never make it out without succumbing to the smoke. And the fire. No, the only way out was the window. He crossed the room, pulling Alyson with him.

She turned to him when they reached the window. "Can we get out this way? Aren't we pretty high off the ground?"

On this side of the house, the window was three stories above the ground, a dormer window set high in the middle of the sloping roof. He peered out the glass. "We don't have a choice."

"We aren't going to be able to jump. There's a brick patio below this window."

"But there's a trellis, as well. If we slide down the roof to the trellis, we'll be able to climb down."

She nodded, as if his plan was logical.

He hoped to God her faith was justified. "With all the rain, the shake roof is going to be slick as ice. We'll need some way to control our descent."

She glanced around him, hurried to the bed and grasped the sheets. "We'll tie these together."

"It's worth a shot." He helped her strip the sheets from the bed and tie them, yanking the knots as tight as he could. When he was satisfied it would hold, he turned back to the window.

He slid the sash up. Fresh air rushed into the

room. They took hungry breaths. So far, so good. The only thing in their way now was the screen. He unfastened the latches and gave the bottom edge a shove. It didn't budge.

Damn. As old as the house, the screens were painted in place.

Fire crackled from downstairs. Dex glanced at the closed door. The air grew thicker with smoke by the second. The rush of fresh air would fuel the fire. He hit the screen's bottom edge with the heel of his hand, again and again.

Finally the paint seal broke and the screen swung into the night, skidding down the shake roof and clattering to the brick patio three stories below.

Alyson handed him the sheet rope. He threw one end outside and tied the sheet to the old iron radiator under the window.

Both coughing from the smoke, he grasped her hand to steady her as she threw a leg over the windowsill. She wore only the T-shirt she'd slept in, her feet were bare. Not ideal clothing for a late-night climb, but it would have to do. There was no way they'd be able to locate her clothing and shoes in the dark. ''The wood shake is going to be slippery, especially with bare feet. Hold on.''

Without hesitation, she hoisted herself outside. She clung to the open window, wind whipping the hem of her T-shirt.

Dex hoisted himself out the window and clung

beside her. The air was clear out here, and he took several deep breaths into his lungs. "I'll go first. That way I can stop you at the bottom." The wood shake cold and slick under his bare feet, he grasped the sheet and gave it a hard tug. It held. So far, so good. He started easing himself down like a mountain climber, letting the sheet slide through his hands. The roar of the waves below filled his ears along with the roar and crackle of fire.

He glanced down. The edge of the roof was getting close now, as well as the end of his bedsheet rope. Nothing but darkness loomed below. As long as the trellis was in the place he thought it was, they'd be all right. If it was more than a few feet to the left or right, he wasn't sure they could reach it on the slick shake shingles.

He glanced up to the window. Alyson clung to the frame, a white spot in the gloom of fog and smoke. He had to be right about the location of the trellis. He had to get them both safely to the ground before the fire licked its way through the old house.

He hastened his steps. His feet slipped on the shake. He fell hard against the roof. The breath exploded from his lungs. Clutching the sheet, he struggled for air. One breath. Two. His lungs ached as he forced the smoky air into them. Slowly, he pulled himself back to his feet. Thank God the knot he'd tied to the radiator had held. If it hadn't, he'd be nothing but a spot on the brick below.

He continued backing down the roof, hand over hand on the sheet rope until he reached the end. Now came the tricky part. If he went over the edge of the roof and the trellis wasn't there, it would be damn near impossible to climb back up.

He lowered himself to his stomach. The moisture from the shake seeped into his clothing. He let himself slide down to the edge of the roof. Lowering himself to the end of the sheet, he tried to feel for the trellis with his feet. It was no use. He would have to let go of the sheet to get low enough to gain a foothold on the trellis. If it was indeed below him.

He sucked in a deep breath and released the sheet. He slid down the shake, the shingles both rough and slick at the same time. His legs went over the edge of the roof. Trying to stop himself, he dug his fingers into the edges of the wood shingles. At the same time, he clawed against the side of the house with his feet.

His feet hit nothing but siding.

He continued to slide. His pulse pounded in his ears. This was it. Either he found that trellis, or he was on his way down to the brick patio. He moved his feet to the side, groping wildly. Finally, his toes hit wood.

He scrambled for a foothold, turning his body to the side to stop his momentum. A piece of the trellis gave way under his thrashing feet. A few inches more. He had to have a few inches more. He strained. His toes caught a piece of solid wood. The edge of the roof dug into his stomach and scraped his skin. He clawed at the shake with his fingers. Just as he was about to go over, he wrenched his body sideways.

Then he plunged over the edge.

He caught the edge of the trellis with his hands. His feet found a hold between vines. He clung there for several seconds, waiting for more of the rotting wood to crumble and send him falling three stories to the brick patio. But it didn't happen. He'd done it. Now he had to get Alyson off the roof, as well.

Summoning his strength, he pulled himself up so he could see over the edge of the roof.

Alyson was still at the window, staring over her shoulder at the spot Dex had disappeared. Smoke billowed out the window behind her. But even through the smoke, fog and darkness, Dex could see tears streaking her cheeks.

He let go of the trellis with one hand and waved. ''Alyson.''

She spotted him, her body almost sagging with relief. She yelled something, but he couldn't make out the words above the intensifying roar of the fire.

He motioned to her to climb down. She nodded and started lowering herself down the incline as he had, her bare feet skidding on the slippery roof.

She fell twice, but held on, lifting herself back to

her feet as if by sheer will. Finally, she reached the end of the sheet rope.

"Get down on your stomach."

She did as he said, flattening her body against the wet wood.

He reached for her and grasped her foot. "Okay, let go and let yourself slide. Slowly."

She released the sheet without hesitating. He guided her slide, pulling her toward him as she went off the edge. She swung into the trellis, slamming into his legs. Dex could feel the wooden grid tremble under the strain, but it held. And so did he.

"I'm on the trellis."

"Do you have a secure foothold? This thing is rotten in places."

"I have it. I'm fine."

He released her hand. The shriek of sirens slashed the night. Above, Dex could see tongues of flame licking the edges of the bedroom window. They climbed down the tangle of wood and vines until they reached the ground.

Once his feet touched brick, he enfolded Alyson in his arms. He held her shivering body tight against him. Tears stung his eyes.

She looked up into his eyes. "When you went over the edge, I thought you were dead. I thought we were both dead."

He smoothed a hand over her wet, tangled hair, careful to avoid the bandage on her forehead. Her sweet scent rose above the stench of smoke and filled his senses. "We aren't dead. We're alive."

"Yes."

He pressed his lips to her hair, taking in the scent of her, the feel of her.

She tilted her head back and slid her arms around his neck. Her lips were so close. So tempting. All he could think about was the feel of them against his. The feel of love. The feel of life. He fitted his mouth over hers.

She accepted the kiss, moving her lips in a dance with his, darting her tongue into his mouth and accepting his. She clung to him as if she would never let him go.

And he didn't want to be let go. She tasted sweet and warm and so accepting. He wanted more. He wanted all of her.

He deepened the kiss, moving his hands over her back and tangling his fingers in her hair. She was so alive. So real. It was as if the time they'd been apart never existed. As if all of it was a bad dream.

The cold finger of reality inched up his spine. The last two years hadn't been a dream. This moment, the feel of her again, the kiss—*this* was the dream.

He pulled away from her. He could feel her eyes on him, but he couldn't return her gaze. And he damn well couldn't explain how he felt. He wasn't even sure himself. "The firefighters are here. We'd better let them know we made it out of the house."

ALYSON WRAPPED the blanket tighter around her shoulders and shivered. The June night wasn't cold. Far from it. And the flame and smoke engulfing Dex's beautiful home upped the temperature at least twenty degrees, even from where they stood across the street.

Dex stood next to her, talking with one of the firefighters about their strategy for saving the house. The flashing red lights from the trucks pulsed off his face. The white dress shirt he wore was rumpled from the day before and wet and dirt-streaked from his slide down the roof. His slacks were ruined and his feet bare. Yet his shoulders were unbowed, as if he was strong as ever, still in charge.

She tried to listen to the firefighter's strategy for salvaging the house, but her mind wouldn't obey. Instead it kept replaying her and Dex's escape from the burning house, the way he'd almost plunged to his death off the roof, the way he'd guided her over the shake and onto the trellis, and most of all, the way he'd taken her into his arms and reaffirmed they were both alive. A flush spread over her skin. Being back in his arms, lost in his kiss, was the only thing that could warm her.

She shook her head. She couldn't let herself think about the way his kiss made her feel, the passion, the tenderness, the need that surged within her like a flame that couldn't be doused. She'd experienced those feelings before. She'd reveled in them. And all they'd given her was shattered dreams and a broken heart.

She forced herself to look away from Dex and to tune into the firefighter's words. "We'll have to wait to find out for certain what caused the fire, but I'd bet my bottom dollar it was arson."

"Arson?" Alyson parroted. She shouldn't be surprised. Houses didn't generally just break into flame without a good reason, even old houses like Dex's. "What makes you think it was arson?"

"The fire moved too fast. Some kind of accelerant had to be used. But we can't say for certain until the fire investigator boys get in there and poke around. They'll be able to tell right away. Then all that will be left is to figure out who struck the match."

The chill spread over Alyson's skin, making her hands tremble. She didn't have to figure out anything. She knew who did it. A glance at Dex confirmed he knew, too.

Smythe.

He'd told Dex he was going to ruin him. Promised he would take everything Dex cared about and leave him with nothing. Of course that list would include Dex's house—the house the two of them had restored from squalor.

She'd felt safe in his house, as if just being inside its walls had swept her back to a simpler time, a happy time. How wrong that feeling was.

A firefighter crossed the street toward them. His stride was urgent. His face was shadowed by the fire and spotlights behind him, but she could see he was young, his pale complexion flecked by soot and ash. He stopped beside the captain. "I need a word with you."

The older man nodded. "Go ahead."

The young firefighter glanced at Alyson and Dex. "Alone."

"Whatever it is, you can say it. Mr. Harrington here is the District Attorney. And Ms. Fitzroy is an analyst at the crime lab."

The young firefighter nodded, but his eyes didn't lose their wary look. "We need to call for additional help. This isn't a simple case of arson anymore."

The captain's busy eyebrows turned down. "Out with it, Franklin."

"We found a body, sir. A woman's body. In the master bedroom. She was on the bed."

Chapter Twelve

Dex pulled a new dress shirt from the closet in his office and ripped open the package. Good thing he kept a half-dozen new shirts and an extra suit in his office. He needed to look presentable for the press conference, and all his clothing had gone up in smoke. Along with his house.

A hollow feeling lodged in his gut. He glanced around his office. Everything seemed the same as yesterday. Alyson sat in the same chair, concern tightening her lips and knitting her brow. Sun bounced off the waves of Lake Monona outside and streamed through his dingy window. And they still didn't have a clue where Smythe had hidden their son.

But this morning everything was different. This morning his house was gone—burned to the ground—and a woman's body had been found in his bed.

They'd stopped at Alyson's house before heading

downtown to the City County Building. There she'd cleaned up, pulled her hair back into some sort of fancy twist, and dressed in a simple black skirt and blouse the same green as her eyes. Now she focused those eyes on him, her complexion so pale the freckles scattered across her nose stood out in sharp relief. "Why don't the police tell us what's going on? Why don't they tell us *anything?*"

Dex stripped off his wet shirt and pulled on the crisp new one. He wished he could reassure her that everything would be all right. That they would get to the bottom of the fire and the murdered woman. That they would find Patrick and put Smythe behind bars. But he wasn't sure of any of those things himself. He wasn't sure of anything anymore. "They probably don't know anything yet."

She glanced at him, shadows of doubt obvious in her eyes. "I've been around law enforcement all my life, Dex. I know when I'm part of the team and when I'm not. And right now, we're not."

"Don't read into it. The cops like to play things close to the vest until they know what they're dealing with. Sometimes that means not communicating everything to the D.A.'s office."

She nodded as if she accepted his answer. But the way she twisted her fingers in her lap told a different story. "I just can't help wondering who she is. And why Smythe killed her. Is she Jennifer Scott? Or is she someone we talked to? Someone he thought we were about to talk to?'' The pitch of her voice rose. ''The woman who was taking care of Patrick?''

He reached in the closet and pulled out a pressed navy suit and silk tie. In fifteen minutes he was scheduled to stand in front of a group of reporters, explain why he was giving up his career, and field whatever queries they tossed his way. And here he could no more answer Alyson's questions than he could answer his own.

He turned and looked into her beautiful green eyes, so desperate, so worried, and shook his head. ''I don't know. I just don't know.''

''WHAT IS YOUR REASON for resigning? The election is only five months away. Why not wait until then?''

Dex glanced around the conference room at the gaggle of reporters and television cameras waiting for his answer. He knew what he had to say. Smythe had all but scripted his answer. The trick was in forcing the words past his lips without choking on them. Focusing on the aggressive blond television news anchor who'd asked the question, he gripped the edge of the speaker's stand and gave her his best attempt at sincerity. ''Thank you for asking that question, Jancy. I've decided to resign because I've let the people I serve down.''

''How did you do that?'' Jancy Brock demanded.

''I made a major mistake. Andrew Clarke Smythe never should have gone to prison. He is innocent.''

The words stuck in his throat like dry plaster. He forced himself to push on. "Instead of serving the people, I let my own personal and misguided bias determine my actions in his case. And it resulted in a man doing prison time for a crime he didn't commit." He glanced away from the blond anchorwoman and found Alyson in the back of the small crowd. Tears sparkled in her eyes and stained her cheeks.

He dragged his gaze from her and focused on the reporters, many with their hands in the air, waiting to prod and probe for tidbits to splash across their articles. He pointed to a male newspaper reporter with bushy eyebrows who'd been relatively soft on him in the past.

"Could your resignation have anything to do with the fire at your home last night?"

"No. I planned to resign long before last night."

"So the fact that the police found a woman's body in your bed had nothing to do with your decision?"

Dex struggled to hide his surprise. The reporter seemed to have as much information as he did about the fire in his own home. He took a calming breath. Maybe he just listened to his police scanner religiously and put the pieces together. "No. I set up this press conference two days ago with the express intent to announce my resignation. Now if there are no more questions—"

The blond anchorwoman's hand shot up.

Dex tried his best not to flinch as he pointed to her. "Jancy?"

"My sources say the woman found in your house was murdered. Do you have any comment about that?"

As far as Dex knew, the police hadn't made that determination. Not for certain. But it was possible a sharp-eared reporter like Jancy Brock could have heard speculation to that effect. "I'm sorry to hear that. But I have no comment. Not at this time."

"And the woman worked in the State Crime Lab. Her name was Jennifer Scott. Can you confirm that for me, Mr. Harrington?"

Dex's mind spun. Jennifer Scott was no longer missing. She was dead. Her body burned to a crisp in his bed. "I have no comment."

"My sources say she worked on the Andrew Clarke Smythe case and that you've been looking for her lately in relation to that case. Is that true?"

Pressure assaulted his chest, making it hard to breathe.

"Are you withholding comment to protect yourself, Mr. Harrington?"

"No. I'm withholding comment because I haven't been briefed on the facts of the case."

"Is the reason you haven't been briefed because the police don't want to share their information with you?"

His voice caught in his throat. He pushed it out in a husky growl. "I'm sorry, Ms. Brock. I can't speculate on things I have no knowledge of."

"Let me reword the question, counselor," Jancy said, her voice thick with sarcasm. "Are the police keeping this information from you because you're a suspect in the murder and the fire?"

Dex's heart froze, then picked up a frantic beat. That was the change he'd been sensing all morning. The change that Alyson had alluded to. The change he hadn't wanted to accept. He wasn't part of the crime-fighting team anymore, but his resignation wasn't to blame. He wasn't briefed on the case because the police suspected him of killing Jennifer Scott and setting fire to his own house to cover up the murder.

He forced himself to meet Jancy Brock's gaze. "I assure you I'm not a suspect."

Jancy smiled, as if she had secret knowledge. Knowledge he'd never be privy to. "That's not the way I heard it, Mr. Harrington. And I have a very reliable source."

A chill raced through him. He found Alyson's eyes in the crowd—eyes that echoed the fear roiling deep in his gut.

DEX CLOSED his office door behind him, wood cracking against wood with the finality of a judge's gavel. By the time this evening's news ended, he'd be accused, tried and convicted in the court of public opinion.

All courtesy of Andrew Clarke Smythe.

He fell into his desk chair. He'd done everything Smythe demanded—he hadn't gone to the police, he'd given up his career—and still the scum had taken his child, his home, his good name and maybe even his liberty. Dex had to figure out a way to fight back. Because he damn well wasn't going to wait around to find out what Andrew Smythe would try to take away next.

A sharp knock reverberated on the closed door. His pulse picked up its tempo. After catching his eye from the crowd, Alyson had wisely ducked into the bathroom before the press conference had broken up. He'd been grateful for her quick thinking. If the reporters had seen them together, who knew what they would dig up for their stories. Memories of Fitz. Or worse, they might discover Patrick.

He sprung from his chair. He hoped she hadn't taken any unnecessary chances in working her way back to his office. But truth was, he couldn't wait to see her. He needed her more now than ever. Needed to see her, to talk to her, to take her into his arms and to feel her body against his.

He opened the door, but instead of Alyson, he looked into the ice-blue eyes and Nordic-fair face of Assistant District Attorney Britt Alcott.

"I'm sorry to bother you, Dex. But we need to talk."

"Come on in." He turned back to his desk, letting Britt close the door behind her.

"I want you to be honest with me." Britt opened in her usual direct way. "Is the governor pressuring you to resign?"

Dex almost gave a sigh of relief. An easy question. One he could answer point blank. He turned to face her. "No. The governor isn't pressuring me."

"Then why—"

"I think the press conference made it clear."

"Clear? The press conference was a fiasco."

Dex folded his arms across his chest. If he had any hope of fighting Smythe's manipulations, he needed answers. And if anyone would be straight with him, Britt would be. "Tell me the truth, Britt. Was it Jennifer Scott in my bed?"

"Yes."

"Am I a suspect in her murder?"

"Officially? I suppose so."

The tension in his shoulders deteriorated into crippling pain.

Britt held up a hand. "Relax, Dex. No one in the office thinks you murdered anyone. I doubt even the police really think you're responsible."

"I was looking for her. Before she showed up dead."

"I know."

"And another woman I was looking for, Connie Rasula, showed up dead up in Minocqua."

She nodded her blond head. "You found her body."

"So you've been briefed."

"Of course I have. But that doesn't mean I think you're a murderer, Dex. The investigation is a formality. No one wants to look like they're playing favorites. Not after Fitz took advantage of the situation the way he did."

A cold feeling settled in Dex's gut. Alyson. "I can't wait to see what the press will do when they catch wind of the fact that Fitz's daughter was with me when we found both bodies."

Britt nodded. "I've heard that. And I imagine soon the media will, too. They're going to have a field day, you know."

Dex balled his hands into fists by his sides. Reporters would be all over Alyson, digging into her past, dredging up her father's crimes. Their whole relationship would take on the appearance of some kind of sordid affair. And Patrick—

Damn Smythe. He'd found a whole new avenue for revenge, all right. A whole new avenue for making Alyson's and his life hell.

"Don't worry," Britt said, her smile stiff with false cheer. "When all the evidence comes back from the labs, you'll be cleared."

"On page seven. Too bad I'll be accused on page one."

"True. But the fact is, you'll be cleared. And this will all fade away."

He wished he could be that certain. Smythe had done a masterful job of manipulating the situation so far. He was beginning to think the rapist-turned-murderer could mold any situation into whatever he wanted. "Let's hope the evidence comes back soon. And that it tells the real story."

Britt's eyebrows lowered and she skewered him with her ice-blue gaze. "Do you care to clear up a few questions I have?"

The questions couldn't be any tougher than the ones he'd already faced. Could they? "Shoot."

"Andrew Clarke Smythe is guilty as sin, and you of all people know it. There has to be an explanation for this DNA test coming back a match. But the explanation is *not* that you railroaded him on a false charge. So what was all that hoopla about at the press conference?"

Dex gave a sigh, but the cause had nothing to do with relief. He should have known Britt wouldn't buy the line he'd fed to the press. He should count himself lucky that half the A.D.A.s in the office weren't lined up behind her, demanding the truth. "Let's just say I have my reasons for resigning."

"Reasons you aren't going to share with me."

"No."

Britt lifted her chin, seemingly satisfied for now. But if Dex knew her, she wouldn't let the subject drop that easily. She was probably just figuring out another strategy for rooting out the truth.

She leaned a slim hip on the edge of a chair. "The governor has asked me if I'd accept the appointment, Dex. He wants me to be the next interim D.A."

Dex nodded. Resigning his office and who would fill his seat was the furthest thing from his mind now. He supposed learning one was a murder suspect tended to reshuffle priorities. "Congratulations. You'll do a great job."

"I don't want the appointment, Dex. You've made a wonderful D.A. since Fitz died. You've turned the office around. You should be behind this desk."

He shook his head. "We both know my political career is over. Even if I'm cleared of all wrongdoing tomorrow, I'll never be able to win an election. People tend to remember scandal. It's sexier than the truth."

Britt's lips straightened into a grim line. "You're probably right. At least tell me why you resigned today. The real reason."

Dex sighed one last time. It was no use. Britt was nearly as stubborn as Alyson. "I'm going through a tough time right now."

She nodded as if to encourage him. "Because of Smythe's release?"

"Yes. But that's all I can tell you. Anything more and I'm afraid I'll draw you into a mess you don't want to be any part of."

"Another scandal?"

He nodded. "A dangerous one."

"Does it have anything to do with why Al Mylinski was shot?"

"Yes."

Anger darkened Britt's eyes. "What can I do to help?"

"Nothing. Al was trying to help. That's why he was shot. I'm not about to put you in that position."

"I'm not a novice when it comes to handling dangerous situations, you know."

Dex remembered. Britt had survived several attempts on her life tied to a case in the past. But that didn't mean he was going to put her in harm's way now. Not unless there was good reason. "If I need your help, I'll let you know."

The chirp of a cell phone cut through the room, staving off Britt's inevitable protest. Dex looked around the room. Alyson's purse perched on his desk blotter, her cell phone peeking out the top.

His gut clenched. Was Smythe making sure the press conference had gone off without a hitch? Or was he calling to taunt Dex about the fire in his house—and Jennifer Scott's murder?

Bracing himself, he reached for the phone, punched the button and held it to his ear. "Yes?"

"Uh, I'm looking for Alyson Fitzroy." A woman's voice came over the line.

Dex glanced at the door. He wanted to talk to Alyson, too. He *needed* to. "This is Dex Harrington. If you'd like to leave a message for Alyson, I'll be sure she gets it."

"Oh, Mr. Harrington. She told me I could also give the results directly to you."

"Results? What results?"

"I'm calling from the State Crime Lab. Alyson asked me to do some additional testing on a blood sample. She said to look for any substance that might be mingled with the blood."

Dex's pulse picked up its pace. He didn't know Alyson had asked for additional tests. But he wasn't surprised she was covering all possible avenues. "Did you find anything?"

"Yes. Something unusual, to say the least."

Dex clutched the phone harder, his grip making the plastic creak. "What?"

"There seem to be traces of a tomato substance mixed with the blood."

"Tomato substance?"

"Yes. It's consistent with ketchup."

Chapter Thirteen

Alyson wrapped her arms around herself and leaned against the bathroom vanity for support. She hated that she'd had to duck out of the press conference before it was over, but she hadn't had a choice.

The questions from the media whirled through her mind. She cringed at the thought of the stories that would no doubt appear on the six o'clock news and in the *Wisconsin State Journal* tomorrow morning. Suggestions that Dex's resignation was linked to the mysterious fire. Suspicions that his search for Jennifer Scott led to her murder. Parallels with her father's crimes and corruption.

And if they found out Alyson had been with Dex the whole time...

So exchanging looks with Dex, she'd slipped out a side door and into the bathroom to wait until the reporters had left. The voices beyond the rest room door had thinned and faded since. Now her problem was to get to Dex's office without being seen. She needed to talk to him, to touch him, to make sure he was all right. And to make sure she was all right, too.

Her body still throbbed with the feel of his solid arms holding her last night after they'd escaped the fire. Her lips still tingled with his kiss. And though they hadn't exchanged a word about the passion and tenderness that had flared between them, she couldn't help but hope it had given them both the strength to get through what they had to do today.

Strength they both sorely needed.

She shivered and tried to push the image of Patrick from her mind. Dex said Smythe wouldn't hurt their baby. But after his brutal slaying of Connie Rasula, the shooting of Al Mylinski, and now Jennifer Scott's murder and the fire, she wasn't convinced he would draw the line anywhere.

Andrew Clarke Smythe had made it clear he was dead set on destroying Dex. But it wasn't until now that Alyson really felt he might succeed.

She focused on the quiet outside the rest room door. Now was her chance. She opened the door and peeked out. No reporters lingered in the halls or the conference room beyond. Slipping out of the rest room, she started in the direction of Dex's office. And stopped dead at the end of the hall. There at the reception desk stood Maggie Daugherty digging through her desk and piling items into a cardboard box.

Alyson gritted her teeth and walked straight for the woman. Getting back to Dex's office would have to wait. If Maggie knew anything about Smythe's location, his plans, and, most of all, where he was hiding Patrick, Alyson wanted to know. If she had to, she'd strangle it out of the woman. "Maggie?"

"I'm awfully busy right now. Can it wait?" Maggie's gaze shifted over the reception area as if she was looking for a way out.

Alyson wasn't about to give her one. "If you want to talk here, that's fine by me."

Maggie's eyes widened. She glanced at the secretaries and paralegals bustling around the office and shook her head. "This way."

She led Alyson into a vacant office and closed the door. "What do you—"

"I want my baby."

"Your baby?"

"Your brother kidnapped my baby. I want him back. And you are going to tell me where Patrick is. Got it?"

Maggie laughed. "If you expect me to believe he's become a kidnapper of babies, you're deluded."

Alyson eyed the woman. She seemed confident. As if she was telling the truth. She couldn't be. "Dex Harrington is my baby's father. Smythe took Patrick for revenge."

The smile disappeared from Maggie's face.

"Just in case you didn't know, your brother has also killed at least two women. And he tried to kill a police detective."

Maggie shook her head. Her bobbed hair whipped against her cheeks. "You're crazy. Andy wouldn't do those things." Her voice rang with conviction. Either the woman should be starring in Hollywood or she really didn't believe Smythe capable of killing.

Alyson narrowed her eyes. "Like he wouldn't rape women?"

She raised her chin in defiance, but she didn't meet Alyson's gaze. "He wasn't guilty of that. The governor pardoned him."

"And how do you think that came about?"

"*Your* test showed the DNA matched the sample from that recent rape attempt and the rapes Andy was convicted for. And Andy was in prison at the time of the recent rape. Dex put away the wrong man."

What Alyson wouldn't give to put her hands around the woman's neck and shake her. Maggie was protecting her brother, that was certain. And Alyson had to break down the woman's defenses. She had to get her to tell where Patrick was. Because Smythe had definitely escalated the stakes in the game he was playing. And she and Dex were out of leads. "Would the wrong man grab me by the throat, threaten me and shove my head into the edge of a table?''

"I never gave you permission to snoop in my house. You surprised Andy. He never would have hurt you otherwise.''

"Like he never would have hurt the other women? The women he raped?''

Maggie's gaze shifted away from Alyson once again.

Alyson took a step toward her. "You can't even look me in the eye. You obviously know he raped those women.''

Maggie's shoulders slumped. She held up a hand. "He's had a hard life. His mother beat him, did you know that? It's only natural he would have a hard time with women. But that's in the past. He's learned his lesson, and he isn't going to do that anymore. He promised me.''

"And you believed him?''

"He promised me on the life of the woman who raised him. He wouldn't do that and not mean it. Besides, he was pardoned for those rapes. He can't be tried for that ever again. That's over.''

"It's not over, Maggie. Not as long as he's out there free. One of the women he murdered since he's been out was Connie Rasula. Did he tell you that?''

Her body jolted with recognition at the name.

"He raped her, then strangled her. Dex and I

found her body at her family's vacation home in Minocqua.''

Maggie shook her head. ''It wasn't Andy.''

''And he shot Detective Al Mylinski while Al was asleep in his bed.''

''Andy couldn't.''

''He could. And he did. And that's not all. Last night he set fire to Dex's house. Dex and I were almost killed. And the firefighters found a woman's body in the master bedroom. It was Jennifer Scott, Maggie. Do you know her?''

Maggie gnawed the inside of her cheek. Apparently brother dear didn't share the details of his day with his sister.

An ache of worry wrapped around Alyson's lungs, making it hard to breathe. If Maggie was the only person Smythe confided in, she would know something of her brother's actions. Wouldn't she? He wouldn't have kept her in the dark totally. ''And your brother kidnapped my son. Dex's and my son. I have to find him, Maggie. I'm afraid he's going to hurt my baby next.''

The last of the color drained from Maggie's face. ''How do I know you're telling the truth?''

''Call the Minocqua police department. Call the hospital and check on Al Mylinski. Watch the news tonight. I'm not lying.''

''I can't believe it. I just can't believe it.''

"Tell me what you know. Please. Before he hurts my baby. Before it's too late. Where's my son?"

"I don't know."

"He just got out of prison. He would have needed help. He can't be taking care of a baby all by himself." Alyson's pulse pounded in her ears. *Unless he wasn't taking care of the baby. Unless Patrick was already dead.*

Pain seized Alyson, nearly doubling her over. Patrick couldn't be dead. He couldn't be. Alyson would feel it, wouldn't she? Wouldn't she know?

She grasped Maggie's arm. She'd shake the truth out of the woman if need be.

A knock sounded on the door. The sound had barely registered in Alyson's mind before the door was pushed open and Dex stepped inside.

"There you are." He looked from Alyson to Maggie, his gaze resting on Alyson's grip on Maggie's arm. "What's going on?"

Alyson pulled a breath of air into her lungs. Thank God, Dex was here. He would help her get to the bottom of this. He would help her force Maggie to tell the truth.

Maggie pulled her arm from Alyson's grasp. Her mouth flattened into a controlled line and her dark eyes hardened with resolve. "Nothing but a bunch of lies. Lies I'm not buying into."

Dex swung the door wide and allowed Britt Alcott into the room. He was so serious. So intense.

And behind him, Britt's elegant face was sharp, as well.

Fear seized Alyson like a strong hand. Her knees felt weak. "What happened?"

Dex pulled his gaze from Maggie and looked into Alyson's eyes. "I got a call from the crime lab. It was about some tests you asked them to perform."

Alyson allowed herself to breathe, scooping oxygen into her hungry lungs. She'd feared the worst, that something had happened, that the police had found Patrick, that he was—

She cut off the thought. She couldn't let herself think that way. If she did, she wouldn't be able to function.

She pulled herself up and took a deep breath. "Did they find anything in the blood?"

He nodded. "Ketchup."

"Ketchup?" she repeated. A cold realization stole over her. "Of course. Ketchup. As in little foil packets ideal for transporting small amounts of blood. As in John Cohen."

Dex's gaze bore into her. "Exactly."

Although she and Dex had tossed around the suspicion that John was involved, she'd never wanted to believe it. She didn't want to believe it now. "John helped Smythe smuggle blood from the prison."

Maggie took a step toward the door. "If you don't need me anymore, I'm going to finish packing up my things. Please pass my resignation along to the next district attorney.''

''Not so fast,'' Dex said.

Behind him, Britt barred the door. A head taller than Maggie, Britt looked down her straight nose. Regal and blond, she looked more like Scandinavian royalty than the hardworking assistant district attorney she was. ''I'm the next D.A. And I need a word with you, Maggie. As soon as Dex and Alyson are done here.''

Maggie looked from Britt to Dex to Alyson. ''If you have evidence John Cohen helped Andy, why do you need me? Why don't you grill John about the things you say Andy has been doing?''

Alyson watched the fear race over Maggie's face, pieces falling into place in her mind. She could still picture John Cohen at the brew pub, grabbing ketchup packets from his briefcase, ripping them open and squeezing them onto his burger and fries when the waitress had forgotten to bring the condiment to his table. ''John didn't help Smythe. He didn't mean to, at any rate.'' She glanced at Dex, looking for his reaction.

He nodded as if following her thoughts. ''John carried the blood out of the prison, but he didn't have anything to do with the scheme. He didn't even know he was carrying Smythe's blood. He, like everyone else, just assumed it was ketchup inside those ketchup packets he has in his briefcase.''

Alyson picked up the thread and ran with it. "And then someone else took the blood from his briefcase while John wasn't looking and hired Connie Rasula to fake the rape."

Alyson glanced at Maggie. The guilt and fear on the woman's face said it all. Alyson brought her gaze back to Dex. "So, Runyon did nothing more than convey messages to and from prison. And Jennifer Scott?"

"I think she merely gave Smythe the notion, if that." Dex tore his gaze from Alyson and turned an accusing stare on Maggie. "But I think we know who did the rest."

Maggie straightened. "I want a lawyer."

He nodded. "You're going to need one."

Alyson focused on Maggie. After the way she'd defended her half brother, the fact she'd helped spring him from prison didn't surprise Alyson in the least. But the last thing she wanted was for the woman to hire some attorney who'd tell her not to say a word. Alyson still hadn't gotten the answers she needed—the most important answers of all. "First tell me about Patrick. Where is he? What has your brother done with him? Please."

Unflinching, Maggie looked her straight in the eye. "I don't know anything about your baby. I swear."

Alyson dropped her gaze to the floor and fought back the tears blurring her eyes. She had no more questions. And no more hope. Because this time, no matter what Maggie had done, Alyson knew in her gut the woman was telling the truth.

DEX WATCHED ALYSON pick at the sandwich he'd bought for her. She usually loved the subs from the local Italian deli. But after today, she probably was having trouble choking down a single bite of food. And he couldn't blame her.

Even though they had discovered the truth behind the DNA double ploy that had led to Andrew Clarke Smythe's pardon, they were no closer to finding Patrick than they were the night Smythe kidnapped him.

Alyson looked up from her untouched sandwich. Circles hovered under her eyes, puffy from tears. "Maggie hasn't said anything more, has she?"

"No. She's following her attorney's advice."

"It doesn't matter."

"Why do you say that?"

"She doesn't know where Patrick is. Smythe didn't confide in her about the things he did after he got out of prison. She was under the impression that her half brother was a swell guy." Bitterness laced her tone.

"Britt will keep working on her. She might give us information in exchange for a reduced charge."

Alyson shook her head. "She doesn't know about Patrick. We've reached a dead end."

Despite his better judgment, Dex reached across the table and touched her shoulder. He wanted to take her into his arms. He wanted to kiss away her fear as he'd kissed the tears from her face last night. He wanted to make everything right again. For her. For Patrick. And for him.

And damn it, he refused to believe they were at a dead end. "If not his sister, who else would he trust to keep a baby for him?"

Alyson's gaze shot to his face, life stirring in her green eyes. "The housekeeper? She was pretty quick to tell us about his relationship with Maggie. Maybe she just wanted to throw us off."

Dex shook his head. "It isn't her. She testified against Smythe at the first trial. Ripped his alibi to shreds. I can't see him ever forgiving her, let alone trusting her to keep a baby stashed for him. She's probably on his revenge list after me."

Alyson's eyes glazed as if her mind was far away. "She said, 'he promised me on the life of the woman who raised him.'"

"What?"

"That's what Maggie said to me. She said Smythe promised her he wouldn't rape again 'on the life of the woman who raised him.' It was the reason she believed he'd stopped."

"He couldn't have meant his mother."

"No. Maggie knew his mother beat him. It had to be someone else. Someone who was good to

Smythe when he was growing up. Someone he cared about—if he's capable of caring about anyone at all. Someone like a nanny.''

Dex jutted to his feet and strode across the room to the bank of file cabinets on the far wall. He pulled a drawer open and rifled the files. "Why didn't I think of it before? If I remember correctly, Smythe had one nanny through most of his childhood."

Locating the file he was looking for, he pulled it from the drawer and spread it open.

Tense as a spring, Alyson followed him to the cabinet and looked over his shoulder at the papers. He could hear her sharp intake of air as she caught her breath and held it.

He flipped through the papers, his fingers beginning to shake. Finally he found what he was looking for. "Here she is. Clara Thompson. And she lives only about a forty-minute drive from here."

ALYSON SHIFTED in the passenger seat of Dex's car and watched the windows of the tiny ranch house. The house, the yard, the whole town looked straight out of a small-town cliché. She glanced down the quiet street. "It's hard to imagine Andrew Smythe having anything to do with such a peaceful town. The neighbors probably leave their doors unlocked."

"Clara Thompson was probably one of the few good influences Smythe had in his life."

"Have you met her?"

"I cross-examined her. She was one of the character witnesses Runyon trotted out as part of his flimsy case."

"So she'll know who you are as soon as she peeks out the door."

"I assume so."

"Then I'll have to go to the door."

He frowned and shook his head. "Not a good idea."

She wasn't about to take no for an answer. "All I need to do is to convince her to open the door. If Patrick is inside, I'm going to find him. Nothing is going to stand in my way. Certainly not an elderly nanny."

"What if Smythe is inside? Do you want to risk a replay of what happened at Maggie's house?"

Alyson's breath hitched in her throat. She hadn't thought about the possibility of Smythe hiding here. Just the thought of his presence in this quiet town was an abomination. "He wouldn't be here, would he?"

"I don't know. But I don't want you anywhere near if he is."

"But if you go to the door, the woman might not even answer the door, let alone invite you inside."

"We'll have to take that chance."

"No. Let me go. You can wait in the bushes near

the house. If Smythe is there, you'll be close enough to use that gun of yours.''

Dex smiled. She might not like guns, but after being attacked by Smythe twice and finding two women murdered by him, she wasn't as averse to the thought of him using it as she'd been only days ago.

"You win." He slipped an arm around her shoulders and pulled her against him. "I'll stay in the bushes until you need me."

She leaned into his warmth, into his strength. She wasn't alone. Dex was here with her. They would find Patrick. They would bring him home. And together they would raise him. Even if they couldn't be husband and wife, they could be Patrick's mother and father. That was all she dared ask for. To have Dex in her life again. To be a family.

Taking a deep breath, she grasped the handle and pushed the door open. She climbed out of the car and smoothed her sweaty hands over her skirt. Before she had the chance to think—to remember Smythe's hands on her, his breath fanning her face—she forced her feet to take one step after another up the street.

She turned onto the sidewalk flanked by moss roses. The sound of Dex's car door opening and the rustle of arborvitae followed her, but she forced herself not to turn around. If she needed him, he'd be there. And that was all she needed to know.

She walked up the narrow walk, her heels clicking on concrete, the only sound in the still summer afternoon. Sweat beaded on her forehead and dampened the hair at the nape of her neck. She climbed the shallow steps leading to the front door and pressed a finger to the glowing doorbell button.

A chime echoed in the house. A few moments later footsteps pattered on the other side of the door. Ruffled sheers pulled back from a side light, and a blue eye peeked out at Alyson. "I'm sorry. I'm not interested in buying anything."

"I'm not selling anything, ma'am." Apparently this snug little community wasn't as naive as it appeared. So much for Ozzie and Harriet stereotypes. The residents of this neighborhood had joined the modern world of crime along with the rest of society.

Or at least the modern world of door-to-door salespeople and evangelists.

Alyson would have to try a tack no kindhearted woman could resist. She infused her voice with all the emotion threatening to break her apart. "I need your help."

"What for?"

"My car has broken down. I need to use your phone to call Triple A."

The blue eye didn't seem to soften. "There's a service station down a few blocks. They can help you there."

So much for hoping Clara Thompson would offer to be a good Samaritan. But the woman had worked her entire life as a nanny, surely Alyson could use that to her advantage. "I can't walk that far. My children are in the car asleep. I hate to wake them. And I can't leave them alone."

The eye withdrew and the sheer fell back into place. A few rattles of locks and the door opened.

The house was dim inside and Alyson had to wait for a moment to let her eyes adjust. Lined seafoam draperies cloaked the windows, blocking the sun. No doubt to keep the seafoam couch from fading. Or the dark green sculpted carpet. And everywhere she looked, upholstery and wood alike were covered with crocheted doilies. It reminded her of visiting her grandmother's house when she was a child.

Clara Thompson stared up at her from her barely five-foot height. Eyes wary, she forced a polite smile to her lips. "You'll have to follow me. The phone is in the kitchen. I don't have one of those fancy ones without the cord."

"I really appreciate this, ma'am. I don't know how I could have handled getting the children to walk one block, let alone several."

"Happy to do it." She nodded matter-of-factly, but she didn't look happy about it. Not happy at all. "How many children do you have?"

Alyson paused to come up with a number. "Three."

The woman nodded, knowingly. Apparently she'd chosen the right one. "The kitchen is this way."

As soon as the woman turned, Alyson took the opportunity to glance around the house. The place was small—tiny really. It shouldn't be hard to find evidence of a baby. Even easier than at Maggie Daugherty's condo. The only drawback was that Mrs. Thompson was painfully neat.

She followed the woman to the back of the house and the kitchen. There on a dish drainer near the sink propped a freshly washed bottle.

A shiver zinged to Alyson's toes.

She motioned to the bottle. "You must have grandchildren."

The woman's smile was genuine this time. "You could say that."

"A baby?" Alyson's legs shook so badly, she leaned against the counter for balance.

"Yes. A boy as sweet as can be."

"I love babies. May I see him?"

Clara hesitated for a moment, then shrugged. "I don't see why not. He just went down for his nap. I'm sure we won't wake him if we just peek in." She squeezed past Alyson and walked back into the narrow hallway.

Alyson forced her trembling legs to follow in Clara's footsteps. Her heart hammered against her ribs. She glanced at the window, searching for a sign of Dex outside. The baby had to be Patrick. It had to be. If it wasn't, Alyson didn't know how she'd control the tears burning behind her eyelids.

Clara opened one of the bedroom doors and stood aside for Alyson to peek in.

Biting her lip, she craned her neck to see around the door. The room was dark and it took her eyes several moments to adjust. The outline of a crib came into focus. Then a little body huddled on the mattress.

And then her child's beautiful face.

"Patrick," she yelled.

Chapter Fourteen

She pushed past the older woman and crossed the room in two strides. Reaching into the crib, she picked up her sweet little boy and kissed his sweet-smelling head. "It's okay, sweetheart. Mommy's here. Everything's going to be all right."

"What are you doing? He's napping. Put him down." Clara's eyes flashed even in the dark room.

Tears blurred the dim room into a mosaic of shadow. "He's my son."

"You're his mother?" Clara barred the door, threatening despite her small stature and feeble age. "You abandoned him. What kind of a woman abandons her own child?"

"Abandoned? He was kidnapped. Stolen from me."

Patrick flailed his hands. His cry split the air.

"Now see what you've done?" Clara advanced. Her hands grasped Alyson's arm.

He was so fragile. So vulnerable. So dependent on his parents to take care of him, to not let him down.

Dex's throat constricted. Plenty of responsibility came with raising a baby. Responsibility his own father had shirked. And even though the moment Dex had heard about Patrick's existence he'd vowed to live up to that responsibility, he didn't have a clue how to begin.

But God, he wanted to learn.

"It's time for him to eat and go to bed." Alyson secured the diaper tape and started clothing the little guy in pajamas sprinkled with yellow bears. Her fingers moved smooth and sure over the baby's clothes, slipping fabric over a limb here, securing a set of snaps there, as if the whole operation was second nature to her. Lifting Patrick from the changing table, she looked up at Dex and smiled through her drape of auburn hair.

What he wouldn't give to smooth that hair back from her face right now, to caress a silken cheek, to take her and their baby into his arms and never let them go. The wife, the family, the complete package. All within his grasp if he could only reach out and claim them.

"Do you want to play with him for a little while?"

He stuffed his hands into his pockets and rocked back on his heels. "He's had a big day. And he's probably hungry. I'll play with him tomorrow."

Alyson cocked her head, an ethereal smile lighting her eyes. "That's right. We have tomorrow, don't we? A lifetime of tomorrows."

Her words cut Dex to the core. A lifetime with Alyson and their son. It sounded like heaven. Or more like a fantasy. It couldn't be reality. Not for someone like him—someone who grew up without a real family, without a stable home.

Could it?

Alyson's telephone rang once, followed by the chirp of her cell phone. A forwarded call.

Smythe.

Alyson's eyes rounded and met his. He could almost see the questions poised on her lips, the fear she didn't want to voice.

"It could be the police," he said, trying to make his voice reassuring.

The phone rang again.

"The kitchen," Alyson whispered. "The phone is in my purse."

He ripped his gaze from her face and ran down the hall and the stairs to the kitchen. Alyson's purse perched on a countertop, the phone inside. He pulled it out and hit the button. "Yes?"

"You shouldn't have messed with me. You should have followed my instructions."

Fury flared inside Dex. "Go to hell, Smythe. It's over. We have the baby."

"I know. Nanny's very upset she lost my son."

Dex gritted his teeth. The thought that Smythe had passed Patrick off as his own grated on his nerves like a boot heel on gravel. As, no doubt, Smythe knew it would. "It's all over, Smythe. We know all about the way you and Maggie used John Cohen to smuggle your blood out of prison. The way Maggie paid Connie Rasula to stage the attempted rape."

"So you've been digging, so what? You aren't going to be able to convince my sister to testify against me. What else do you have?"

"The deaths of Connie Rasula and Jennifer Scott."

"The way I heard it, the police like you for those murders. At least that's what was all over the evening news."

Dex gritted his teeth. So Jancy Brock had gone ahead with her story. Dex's career as district attorney really was over.

Alyson entered the kitchen. Face pale, she clutched Patrick tight, as if afraid Smythe could reach him over the phone lines.

Dex gave her his best imitation of a smile. Somehow just looking at her holding their son made sacrificing his career lose its sting.

"Can't think of anything else, huh?" Smythe's smug voice snaked into his thoughts. "You forgot that detective. What's his name? Mylinski? Though I understand he hasn't died—yet."

And he wasn't going to. Mylinski was growing stronger every day. Not that Smythe needed to know that. "We'll add attempted murder to your charges. Arson, too."

"But where's the evidence?"

"The police have plenty of evidence against you for kidnapping."

"Oh? How can I kidnap my own baby?"

"You might have been able to fool your elderly nanny, but you won't fool anyone else."

"Who's to say he's not mine? There's no father listed on the birth certificate. Did you know that? Short of a DNA test, you can't prove the kid is yours, any more than I can, Harrington."

"Or we could just make it easy and ask the mother."

"If she's alive to tell the tale."

Rage screamed in Dex's ears. Anger pounded with each beat of his heart. He was sick to death of Andrew Clarke Smythe. And now that they'd found Patrick, he didn't have to play his twisted games anymore. "It's just a matter of time before the police find you, Smythe. The next time I see you, I'll be in the witness box testifying about the things you've done."

His laugh grated over the phone line like a string of profanity. "I wouldn't count on them finding me.

Not yet. I'm not done with you. And I'm certainly not done with the redhead. You're still in my reach.''

"Go to hell, Smythe."

"Been there. But I'd love to give you a tour. Pleasant dreams.'' The phone line went dead.

Damn. Dex punched off the phone and pounded his fist on the countertop the way he wanted to pound Smythe's smug face.

"What did he say?'' Alyson searched his face, her skin as white and fragile-looking as tissue.

"The usual. How he's not done with us. How we are still in his reach.''

"Are we?''

"I don't see how. The police have this place surrounded.''

"And they'll keep it up until he's caught?''

"He's getting desperate. Sloppy. They'll catch him soon.''

"And if they don't?''

"Then we'll get you and Patrick out of town. Somewhere Smythe can't find you.'' As the words left his lips, emptiness ached in his chest.

"I don't want to leave, Dex. I want to stay here. With you.''

He knew how she felt. Knew it far too well. And he didn't want to stay with her for a night or a week or a month. He wanted to believe he could live in the fantasy for the rest of his days.

If only his past and Andrew Clarke Smythe would let him.

ALYSON STOPPED at the entrance to the living room. The room was dark, but she knew Dex was inside. Pausing a moment to let her eyes adjust, she spotted him. He stood at the front window. Holding a section of the sheers aside with one hand, he stared into the darkness outside. Tension hardened his shoulders, visible even under the crumpled dress shirt.

She wanted to slip behind him and massage the hard muscles. She wanted to feel the warmth of his skin under the crisp cotton, the knotted muscles slowly succumbing to her fingers. She wanted to lose herself in the masculine scent of him, so close, so real.

While Patrick was in Smythe's hands, she hadn't been able to think of anything but finding him, of holding him close again, of ensuring his safety. But now that he was safe in his bed, thoughts and feelings swirled within her like dangerous currents.

She wasn't worried about Smythe and his threats. Not really. Dex had reassured her that he would never be able to get past the police outside. No, she was more worried about herself. And her feelings for Dex.

Since Dex had written her off fifteen long months ago, she'd focused on putting herself back together and protecting herself from ever being hurt again. But in the past few days, she'd forgotten what she was protecting herself from.

Taking a breath of courage, she stepped into the room and crossed the plush carpet. Although Dex didn't glance back from his vigil, he knew she was there. She could hear it in the speeding of his breathing pattern and feel it in the charged air.

"Did you get the baby to bed?"

It was such an innocent question, a natural question, yet the low rumble of his voice caused a warm stirring in the pit of her stomach. "He was tired. He went to sleep before he finished nursing."

He nodded, the light from the hallway glinting in the gold of his hair.

Alyson stepped toward him as if pulled by a force she couldn't control. Stopping behind him, she slipped her hands on either side of his neck and began to knead the hard muscle with her fingers.

He held up a hand. "Alyson, don't."

She stopped kneading, but left her hands in place, soaking up the heat through his wrinkled shirt. "You look so tense."

Slowly he turned to face her. A crease formed between his penetrating blue eyes and tiny lines rimmed his lips. The hall light reflected off his glasses, hiding his eyes.

But she didn't need to see his eyes to know what he was feeling. It was the same thing she was feeling. The yearning, the heat she'd seen rekindle in his eyes over the past few days. The passion she'd felt in his kiss after they'd escaped the fire. She dropped her hands to her sides.

"You're right. I am tense."

"Why?"

He looked away from her. "I don't know. Smythe's call I guess."

"You said that even if he was obsessed enough to try something, he wouldn't get past the police outside."

"He won't."

"Then we're safe, aren't we? And Patrick is safe, too."

He looked back into her eyes. "Yes. We're safe from Smythe."

She said nothing. She didn't know what else to say. They both knew where the danger lay. And it wasn't somewhere outside her house. It was here. In this room. And it stretched between them like a minefield.

"You're really good with Patrick, you know. A natural mother."

"Thank you. It wasn't always easy." As soon as the words left her lips, she wanted to take them back. He'd take them the wrong way. He'd blame himself. "But it was always worth it. I'm just glad I can finally share him with you."

His lips curled in a solemn smile. "It's amazing."

"What is?"

"That the two of us created him. It's a miracle."

She nodded, unsure her voice would function. In the long months she carried Patrick inside her, she'd often dreamed of Dex saying something like this to her. That their baby was a miracle, that he was the culmination of their love. And in her imagination he'd always followed that pronouncement by asking her to come back to him, to marry him so the three of them could be a real family. "I miss you, Dex."

A muscle flexed along his jaw. "Don't go there, Alyson. Please."

She shook her head. As much as she wanted to do as he asked, to stay safe and avoid her feelings, to bury them in the ground until they turned to dust, she couldn't. "I know you can't forgive me. I know you can't promise me anything. But I see the look in your eyes, Dex. And you want the same things I do. The things we always used to want."

He took a step away from her, as if he was going to pace across the room. But he didn't take the next step. "Hell, Alyson, there's nothing to forgive. But as much as I want to, I can't go back."

"I don't want to go back, either. I want to go forward, if we can. I want to give us a chance. A chance we never really had before."

"Never really had?"

She bit her bottom lip. How could she explain her feelings to him? The uneasiness of never being certain where she stood? The fear that one day he'd write her off for something she'd never foreseen? "Even when we were happy, I was never sure where I stood with you. I always felt that I had to watch every step I took or you'd write me off."

"Like I wrote you off when you sided with your father."

"Exactly. Being with you was like walking a tightrope. And I never knew my feet had slipped from the rope until I was on my way to the floor of the big top and you'd stopped loving me."

"Alyson, I never stopped loving you."

A chill shook her from the inside out.

"I just couldn't let myself show it. I couldn't let myself take you back."

"Like your mother took your father back?"

He shook his head. "Like *I* took my father back. It wasn't just my mother who forgave him. I wanted him to be the man he should have been. I never gave up wanting that. I never gave up believing in him. And I know damn well that was the main reason my mother stayed with him. She didn't want to disappoint me."

A chill climbed up Alyson's spine. She reached for Dex's hand. "You were a kid, Dex. You can't take that kind of responsibility on yourself."

"It's the truth. I may not have caused my mother's death, but I did contribute to it. My dreams and fantasies of having a father contributed to it.

And as a result, I lost both her and my father for good.''

The pain in his eyes stole her breath. She swallowed into a raw throat.

His fingers closed around hers and squeezed. "It's not that I can't trust you. I can't trust that what I'm feeling is real and not just the way I want things to be. And I can't risk hurting you if I'm wrong.''

"What I feel is real, Dex. I love you.''

Reaching a hand to her face, he traced her jaw with a feather touch, stopping when he reached her lips. "I'm sure what you feel *is* real. But then you've always been much more sure of yourself. You've always known what you want out of life.''

"I wanted you, Dex. All of you. Forever. Without reservations. And it's what I want now.''

He shook his head. "I don't know if I can give you that.''

She looked into his eyes, so tortured, so sad. Maybe he was right. Maybe he couldn't give her what she wanted, what she needed. Maybe she would never be sure of his love, never be sure he would stay with her, that she would never be alone again. Maybe he would leave her heartbroken and battered.

But none of it mattered.

"I love you, Dex. And I want you. If that means we can only be together for a night or a week or an hour, so be it. I'll take it and feel I'm the luckiest woman on earth.''

Chapter Fifteen

Dex watched Alyson's lips purse together, her eyes searching his face as if looking for answers. She'd sounded so sure of herself, so sure of her offer to him. But he could tell inside she was as unsure as he was.

"Dex?" Her voice was tremulous, no more than a whisper, and it hung in the air between them.

He ran his fingertips along her cheek. She was so soft. So vulnerable. And at the same time, strong as iron.

God, he wanted her.

The fantasy couldn't last. He knew it. Not for Alyson and not for him. But maybe for this one night, that didn't matter. Maybe for this one night they could live in the fantasy and let all the rest fall away. Maybe for this one night they could be happy. "I want to make love to you, Alyson. I've wanted to for so long."

A smile spread over her lips. Lips he wanted to touch, to kiss, to claim.

Fire curled inside him. He'd tried not to think of their past together, back when they were happy. He'd tried not to let himself remember. He'd been struggling since the night she'd shown up on his doorstep and told him they had a son. But now with her standing in front of him, her eyes darkened to jade with passion, he didn't need to relive memories. The dream was right here. Right now. A dream he wanted to lose himself in.

He cradled her face in his palms, burying his fingers in her hair. Her skin was like satin, her hair silkier and more lush than in his memories. His fantasies.

She closed her eyes, her lashes brushing pale cheeks. Her lips parted, soft and ready for his kiss.

Lowering his head, he angled his mouth to fit over hers. The first touch of her lips stole his breath, the second seared his soul.

Her arms circled his shoulders, pulling him closer, tighter. He thrust his tongue into her mouth, joining with hers, his kiss hard and demanding, like the need pounding inside him. And she answered with the same ferocity. As if she couldn't get enough.

He remembered thinking how fragile she looked. Yet the woman kissing him now was far from fragile. She wanted this as much as he did. Needed it. And knowing that fired his blood past reason.

He skimmed his hand through her hair and over her shoulders. His fingers found the buttons of her blouse. One by one, he slipped them free, loosening the silken fabric to expose the silkier skin underneath. Without releasing her lips, he glided the blouse off her shoulders and arms and let it fall to the floor.

She shivered, goose bumps rising on her skin.

He ran his hands over her arms. "Cold?" The question slipped out between kisses.

"No. I just want you close. Need you close. I want your skin on mine." She clawed at the buttons of his shirt.

Grasping the collar of his shirt, he ripped, popping the buttons free. Then he pulled her tight to his bare chest. Circling his hands around her back, he found the clasp of her bra. Fingers suddenly clumsy as a teenage boy's, he worked the hooks loose and slipped the bra off between their bodies.

Her breasts spilled free, their weight pressing against his chest, the warmth of her skin burning into him.

He released her lips. "I want to look at you. I want to remember everything about you, about this night." He stepped back from her.

The dim light from the front hall caressed her pale skin. Her breasts were so beautiful, fuller and riper than before, swelled with nurturing their son. The son they had conceived together. "You're so beautiful. Like a dream.'' He gathered her close, slipping his hands over her soft mounds, cupping their abundance. Her nipples were larger, as well. They stood out as if begging him to take them into his mouth.

And he couldn't resist. He cupped a heavy breast in his hand, lowered his mouth to her and gently kissed the nipple.

She moaned and arched her back.

He found her other breast with his hand, holding, caressing. He closed his lips around her nipple, teasing it with his tongue as he sucked.

Sweetness filled his mouth, the taste of her, the essence. He sucked one breast, then the other, the flavor of her milk washing through him, rinsing him clean.

Her fingers combed through his hair. She bent and pressed her lips to his forehead in a gentle kiss. A kiss that took his breath away.

She peeled his shirt from him. Cool air rushed over his skin, making her heat all the more delicious, all the more compelling. Her fingers smoothed over his back, his stomach, stoking his desire. Desire so long denied.

He raised his head and captured her lips. She opened her mouth for him, and he thrust his tongue inside, taking, claiming. She matched his hunger, his need. Deepening the kiss, she pulled him down onto the couch, his body over hers.

He wanted to be closer, to touch her, to claim her.

He found the hem of her skirt and pushed it up her thighs until it bunched around her waist.

Then she was helping him, pushing down her panty hose and opening her thighs.

He slipped his hands between her legs. She was warm and wet for him, as eager for him as he was for her. He caressed her, gently at first, then building in intensity until she arched her back and pressed against him. A moan slid from her lips.

Her hand found the waistband of his slacks. She unfastened his belt and lowered the zipper. Pushing beneath the elastic of his briefs, she slipped her hand around him and cradled him with gentle fingers.

He was plenty hard before she touched him. But with the embrace of her fingers, he thought he'd explode. He wanted to bury himself inside her. To lose himself in her warmth. In her love. In the dream.

She moved her fingers over him, stoking the fire until he couldn't stand it another moment. He grasped her hand, stilling her movement and hurriedly divested her of her panty hose and himself of his pants.

She pressed a hand on his chest, pushing him back against the couch. In one movement she straddled him. Her hand found him, holding him, positioning him. And then she lowered herself to him.

He thrust upward, meeting her, sinking into her. Their gasps mingled. She clung to his shoulders, her breasts surging into his face. He held her against him, his lips skimming over her breasts, devouring her nipples.

She arched her back. Pressing her lips to his forehead, she raked her fingers through his hair. "Dex." His name sounded primitive on her lips, so full of need, of desire.

And his desire answered, so long repressed.

The muscles in her thighs tightened against him. He grasped her hips, raising and lowering her over him, sinking deeper with each stroke, until they were joined together, melded by the heat, and he couldn't tell where he left off and she began.

A sound escaped her lips. A murmur low in her throat. Her breathing grew ragged. She grasped his shoulders, her fingernails digging into his flesh.

He drove into her, her softness sheathing him again and again. Her body convulsed in an intimate embrace. And his body answered. He poured himself into her, his strength, his judgments, his fears. And she accepted it all, without question, and gave back nothing but love.

Love.

And he loved her, too. He always had.

Even those long months when they were apart. Even when he was angry over the choices she'd made. Even now when the future was so uncertain. He loved her. She was his fantasy, his dream.

And more than anything, he wanted to get lost in that dream and never wake up.

ALYSON CURLED INTO Dex's embrace, her back pressing against his chest. His arm draped over her, his hand cupping her breast. Sun glowed through the window, almost as bright as the glow inside her. After they'd made love the first time, they'd checked on Patrick and retired to her bedroom with the intent to sleep. But once they'd climbed into bed, they soon realized sleep was the furthest thing from their minds.

A smile spread over her lips, and warmth curled around her heart. It had been too long since Dex had touched her. Too long since she'd felt so alive, so sated, so loved. Too long since she'd felt anything but endless loneliness. But last night all of that had fallen away. The judgment, the hurt, the loneliness. And they'd been left with nothing but each other.

Nothing but their love.

It was as she always hoped it could be. She snuggled closer to soak up just a little more of his heat.

''Good morning.''

She flipped onto her back and looked into his blue eyes. ''I didn't realize you were awake. Why didn't you say something?''

His hair was tousled, making him look like a beach bum enjoying life. So different from the past days. The past years. "I was enjoying watching you sleep."

"I don't want to hear one word about my snoring."

He smiled, his blue eyes as bright as the sky outside the window. "Don't worry. I won't hold it against you. It's actually kind of cute." Placing one hand on either side of her face, he tilted her chin back and claimed her lips.

His kiss was warm and sweet and held nothing back. She pressed her body against his under the sheets, naked skin to naked skin. She could feel his erection stir and press against her thigh.

He ended the kiss and looked into her eyes. "You'd better be careful. We'll never get out of this bed."

"That suits me just fine. But unfortunately there's no danger of that happening."

"You underestimate me."

"No. You underestimate our son. He should be waking up any minute now." She glanced in the direction of the hall leading to Patrick's room and then shot Dex a teasing grin. "Disappointed?"

"A little. But I can't wait to see him."

As if on cue the baby monitor at the head of the bed erupted in a tiny wail. "Sounds like you got your wish." She tossed back the sheets and climbed from the bed.

He skimmed her bare skin with an appreciative

gaze. "If I'd known I'd get a show and a baby, I'd have made my wish sooner."

"A show?" She raised a brow. "You mean, now you get to see my stretch marks in the sunlight."

"Didn't I tell you how much stretch marks turn me on?" He continued his perusal of her body.

Warmth spread over every inch of skin his gaze touched. His teasing and the naked appreciation in his eyes made her feel truly sexy for the first time since she'd given birth. She padded to the bathroom on bare feet, grabbed her robe from the hook on the back of the door, and slipped it on.

"Censor," Dex said.

She couldn't keep the smile off her face. "If you stay right where you are, maybe you'll get another glimpse." She strode out of the room and down the hall in the direction of Patrick's room. All the endless months she and Dex had been apart, she hadn't been able to give up hope that someday they'd be together like this. Like they were last night. No judgments, no bitterness, nothing but love between them. And her hopes had been realized. All she had to do was look into his eyes to know she wasn't alone anymore. And now that Patrick was back safe and sound, they'd all be together. A family.

When she entered the room, Patrick let out a squeal. He rolled to his tummy and lifted his head from the mattress to peer through the crib rails.

"Good morning, sweetheart." She crossed the

room and lifted him from the crib. Snuggling his little body close, she kissed the top of his head and breathed in his sweet baby scent.

Tears clogged the back of her throat. He really was home. Safe. And nothing could change that. She wouldn't let it. She laid him on the changing table and changed his diaper, her fingers moving with the deftness of a well-remembered ritual. When he was clean and dry, she gave him a bright smile. "Do you want to go see Daddy? He can't wait to see you."

His little face puckered into a frown. A whimper escaped his lips.

"And you can eat breakfast, too. Don't worry."

She carried him back down the hall, to where Dex was waiting, propped against the headboard. Soft light filtered through the curtains and glowed on his bare chest. The sheet pooled around his waist. A smile lifted his lips and reflected in his eyes, outshining the brilliance of the sun.

"Here's the little man." She laid Patrick on Dex's chest, circled the bed and climbed under the sheets next to him.

Dex held Patrick close, looking at him as if he'd never seen anything so incredible in his life.

Patrick's little face collapsed into a grimace. Then an outright frown. A protest rose from his lips.

Dex shot Alyson a helpless look. "He really does

look like me, doesn't he? When I'm in a bad mood.''

She couldn't help but laugh. ''He's not in a bad mood. He's just hungry.'' She took Patrick from Dex and loosened her robe. He latched on to her breast with a voracious hunger and started nursing. He hadn't forgotten how, just as he hadn't forgotten his mommy.

Dex circled his arm around her shoulders and pulled her close while Patrick nursed.

She laid her head against his shoulder. She'd lied to herself last night. And she'd lied to Dex. She told him she'd be happy with whatever he could give her, whether it was one night, one week, or one hour. But she'd never be happy with anything less than this. What she saw in his eyes and felt in her heart. What they had right now.

She looked up at him. His attention was turned to the window, a faraway look in his eyes.

''Tell me what you're thinking.''

A smile flitted over his lips. ''I was thinking that this is a dream, you and me and Patrick. A dream I never want to wake from.''

A chill inched up her spine. Last night he'd talked about the difference between what he wanted to believe concerning his father and what was real. ''What we have is no dream, Dex. It's as real as this bed. As these sheets.''

He touched a finger to her forehead, smoothing

loose strands of hair back from her face. "It's just as good as a dream. I never knew it could be so good."

"But?"

A furrow dug between his brows. "But nothing. I love you."

A familiar ache settled in her chest. Maybe she was being paranoid. Maybe it was her imagination. Dex was still here in bed with her, with Patrick. He'd told her he loved her. Nothing had changed since the moment before.

But everything had changed.

"What's wrong, Alyson?"

She blew a breath through tense lips. "Maybe nothing. I don't know."

"Care to explain?"

"Last night you talked about how you dreamed your dad would be a good person someday, but in reality he fell short."

"He did."

"Yes. And the same thing happened with my father, too, didn't it? You wanted him to be a man you could look up to, a mentor. But he didn't live up to the dream you had of him."

"What are you getting at?"

"I don't want to be another dream, Dex. Not this time."

He tightened his arm around her shoulder. "I

didn't mean it that way. I just meant that what we have is so good it doesn't seem real."

"But that's just it. Don't you see? I can't live up to the fantasy. Sooner or later I'll disappoint you, like I did last time we were together."

"Last time was about your father, what he did."

"No, it wasn't. Not totally. It was about us, too. It was about you writing me off as soon as I disappointed you. As if you were waiting for me to let you down the way your father and my father did. I'm not walking that tightrope again, Dex. I can't. And Patrick isn't going to walk it, either."

Throwing back the sheets, he swung his legs over the edge of the bed. She expected him to stand and pace across the room. It had always been his way of escaping something that was bothering him. But he remained on the bed. Sunlight through the curtains cast soft shadows across his muscled back.

She swallowed into an aching throat. "I thought things were different this morning, that everything had changed. But I was wrong. We're still the same people. And we still carry the same baggage."

"I want things to be different. *I* want to be different." Anguish laced his voice and twined around her heart.

She wrapped her arms tighter around Patrick, holding on for dear life. "You have to believe you deserve happiness. You have to believe happiness is more than just a dream."

He turned to face her on the bed. "I want to. Believe me. But I don't know if I can. I don't even know how to start."

"I can't tell you how, Dex. That's up to you. You either do it or you don't."

He turned away from her and buried his face in his hands.

Her throat closed and tears stung her sinuses. She loved him so much she ached. But what good did it do? "Last night I told you I'd be content with whatever you wanted to give me, a night, a week, or even an hour. But I was wrong. I want all of you. And if I have to choose between sitting around waiting for the dream to end or being alone, I'll have to be content with being alone."

DEX DESCENDED THE STAIRS and strode through the foyer and into the kitchen. He had showered and shaved, but the hot water and steamy bathroom had done nothing to clear the anguish tumbling through his mind.

Alyson sat at the kitchen table spooning some sort of baby food into Patrick's mouth. She looked up as he entered. Sunlight streamed through the open windows, highlighting the freckles scattered across the bridge of her nose like the spots on a fawn and sparking her hair to red flame. It was the perfect domestic picture, a beautiful mother caring for her child. Only the sorrow in her eyes and the creases around her lips spoiled the effect. ''What are you going to do?''

Damn good question. What *was* he going to do?

If only he could fall on his knees, insist she was wrong about him and ask her to be his forever. But he couldn't. Because as much as he didn't want to admit it, she was right.

His heart seized in his chest. He couldn't lose Alyson. Not now that he'd found her again. And he didn't want to go through the rest of his life alone, not trusting his own feelings, never knowing if they would change the moment reality intruded. But Alyson was right. He couldn't put her through that, not again. And he damn well couldn't subject Patrick to that kind of uncertainty.

He peered out the window at the sun-stained day. An unmarked police car sat parked in the neighbor's driveway, the outlines of two officers dark against the brilliant sun. From their vantage point, they could easily see the entire back and sides of Alyson's house. He'd seen the other car out front this morning after his shower. At least he didn't have to worry about security this morning. There was no way Smythe could worm his way past that kind of scrutiny. And even if he somehow managed it, the security system Dex had had installed would alert police before the scum had a chance to step over the threshold.

Alyson was still watching him, waiting for an answer.

He met her gaze. "I'm going to leave. At least for a while."

She nodded as if she expected his answer. Worry lines etched her forehead and flanked her lips.

"Don't worry. You and Patrick will be safe here." He gestured out the window. "The police have turned this place into a fortress. No one could get in without their knowing it."

"I saw them. I'm not worried about that. I'm worried about you."

"I'll be fine. Smythe won't hurt me. Not yet. He hasn't finished making me suffer."

"I'm not just talking about Smythe."

No. He knew she wasn't. "I'll be okay. I always am."

"Where are you going?"

Another good question. "I'm going back to the source."

THE SOFT mechanical roar of the garage door lifting filtered through the floorboards and echoed in the concrete basement. Andrew Clarke Smythe looked toward the sound and smiled. He'd been waiting for this moment for days—no years. The moment of his revenge. And it was almost here.

It was about damn time.

He stretched out on the pitiful, lumpy couch he'd

spent the night on. It had been good of Nanny to call him the moment Harrington and the redhead found the kid. She'd been so worried, the poor old bat, fit to be tied. She hadn't understood he really didn't care about the baby, that the kid was no more than a tool, a way to manipulate the father.

He hated to lose that tool, of course. It had been fun wielding that much power over Harrington. But he'd manage just fine without the kid. Especially now that he was in place for his next move.

He propped his athletic shoes on the scarred coffee table in front of him. All he had to do was sit back and wait for the car to start and back down the driveway. For the garage door to close behind it. For his hunger for revenge to build toward its lustful climax.

Closing his eyes, he tried to picture Alyson Fitzroy. The chilly sound of her voice. The superior glint in her eyes. The way she stood with her chin up and her chest thrust out like she was challenging the world. Like she was better than everyone else.

He smiled.

She wouldn't be chilly and superior with him. He wouldn't allow it. His fingers itched to grasp that long, red hair, to strip off her clothes, to put the bitch in her place and to show her what revenge was *really* all about.

But that wasn't all. This time he had a little extra planned. Alyson Fitzroy wouldn't be like the others. He'd changed since he'd gotten out of prison. He'd grown. And his ambitions had grown, too. He'd enjoyed silencing Connie Rasula and Jennifer Scott. He'd enjoyed closing his hands around their throats. He'd enjoyed squeezing the life out of them at the same time he'd pounded his rage into them.

And with Alyson Fitzroy he would be so much more—more brutal, more demeaning, more deadly. He'd been thinking up ideas for days. And he'd try out every single one. After all, she deserved it. She and Dex Harrington deserved everything he could give them.

The car purred to life in the garage and backed out. The door whirred closed, and all that was left was silence. Andy looked around the basement rec room, the shabby couch, the paneled walls, the corner filled with boxes. Harrington and the redhead thought they were out of his reach. They thought he could never get past the police protecting the house. They thought he could never breech the security system. They thought they were perfectly safe in their little love nest.

But Alyson Fitzroy was far from safe. Not while he was around. A mere twenty thousand dollars had convinced the technician who'd installed the security system to give him the code. And even if the entire Madison police department was milling around outside the house, they couldn't protect the redhead. Because Andy didn't need to break through a police perimeter to get into her house.

He was already here.

Chapter Sixteen

Dex lowered himself into a wooden chair and glanced around the shabby living room. Back when he was an assistant district attorney trying cases, he'd visited a number of the halfway houses in Dane County to question witnesses. But he'd never stepped inside this particular one.

It looked comfortable, if living with eight fellow felons could be considered comfortable. His father had served his sentence for involuntary manslaughter by use of a motor vehicle a number of years ago, but that didn't mean he'd reformed. The drunk driving hadn't magically stopped. Neither had the petty theft. He'd even visited his old cronies in prison when he'd stolen a junker and gone for a drunken joy ride. A combination of all his talents.

Although Dex hadn't seen his father since his mother died, that didn't mean he hadn't kept tabs on the old man. And it didn't mean he'd been immune from further disappointment, either.

He sure as hell hadn't given his son much to be proud of.

"Hello, Dex."

A chill ran up his spine. For all his drinking and smoking, the old man still sounded the same as when Dex was a boy. His voice was low, almost sweet. A voice that could charm the sun out from the clouds, his mother had always said. But it didn't have that effect on Dex. Not anymore. Now it just made his gut clench with anger. "I need to talk to you."

The old man shuffled to the chair opposite Dex at the scarred table. His face was lined beyond his years. His hair was coarse and gray and stuck out from his head in unkempt clumps. Unlike his voice, his youthful appearance and sandy-blond hair had become victims of booze and smoke. But even sagging skin and two days' growth of silver beard couldn't camouflage the chiseled jaw, the cleft chin, so like Dex's. And so like Patrick's.

The old man's lips crooked into a grin, exposing stained teeth. "Finally come to see your dear old dad, eh? It's about time you acted like a son."

Dex clenched his hands into fists under the table. What he wouldn't give to launch himself over the table, to drive his fists into that smug old face, to take out the years of grief and guilt and bitterness on the man who inspired it. "Believe me, if I had a choice I wouldn't be your son."

"Funny how we don't have that choice, eh?" The old man had the nerve to chuckle. "Now spit it out. What could you possibly want with me after all these years?"

What *had* he come for? What did he hope this meeting would prove? That he could forgive his father? That he could forget what the old man had done to his mother? To him? There wasn't a chance in hell of that happening.

What, then?

"I wanted to see you. I wanted to look into your face and know that I'm nothing like you."

"No can do. You're a regular chip off the old block, sonny boy."

Dex took a deep breath and willed himself to remain seated. "I'm nothing like you."

"You can't B.S. a B.S.er, son. I can see me in your eyes just as clearly as I could fifteen years ago." He shrugged his bony shoulders. "Sure, you don't drink and you don't steal and all that other crap they've been saying I do. But you're hard, my boy. Just like me. Like I said, I can see it."

"If I am, it was you that made me hard."

"Guilty as charged. Isn't that what you lawyer types say? And who do you think made *me* this way? You ever think about that?"

No. He hadn't. And he didn't care to think about it now. Knowing his father, he'd only pin the blame on Dex or his mother or society in general. "You made yourself that way, old man."

"You may be right about that. And if that's true, you have only to look in the mirror to find who made you."

Uneasiness clamped down on Dex's shoulders. Had he chosen bitterness the way his father had chosen booze? Was judging others as addictive to him as alcohol to an alcoholic?

He shook his head. His father was damn good at turning everything around, making Dex blame himself for anything the old man did. Just as he'd made his mother feel as if she'd failed him. "Did you feel anything when Mom died? Did it even register that you'd killed her?"

His father flinched as if Dex had reached across the table and hit him. "You leave your mother out of this."

"I'm not talking about Mom. I'm talking about you. Did you ever face the fact that you killed her? That it was your fault she died?"

"I faced everything I needed to face. I had six years to do nothing but think about it, remember?"

"Not long enough. Six years doesn't make up for her death. Not even close."

"No. There ain't enough prison time in the world to make up for that."

At first, Dex wasn't sure he'd heard the old man right. He'd offered no excuses, shifted no blame. He sat back in his chair and watched his father through narrowed eyes.

The old man clawed a hand through his gray hair. "I only wish your precious court system had done its job."

"There it is. The excuses. The blame shifting. For a second there I thought you might have changed. Just a little. But you're just as pitiful as you always were. You're just getting craftier at avoiding fault."

"I'm not shifting blame. I'm stating fact. If the courts had put me away when they should have, I never would have been driving the car that night. And your mother would still be here." His voice cracked. Tears pooled in his eyes. "I know it's my fault she's dead, Dex. It's something I'll never forgive myself for. I deprived you of a mother. And I deprived the world of an angel."

Dex's lungs ached as if he'd just had the wind knocked out of him. He tried to recover, to drag oxygen into his lungs, but he couldn't. He couldn't do anything but stare at his father's face and listen.

"Your mother was the rarest of all people—a woman who loved unconditionally, who forgave without question, who lived life with grace. You and me are alike, Dex. But there's one big difference. We both had scoundrels for old men, but my mother was little more than a whore. You lucked out. An angel raised you. And if I could wish for anything in this world besides bringing her back, I'd wish that you'd grow up to be more like her.''

Dex sat and stared, his body numb. His old man was right. Dex had spent his life trying to punish his father, to get revenge against his father with every defendant he put behind bars. And in doing so, he had forgotten totally about his mother, about the example she set, about the woman she was.

''I had a good thing with your mother, Dex. Something so good, I couldn't let myself believe it. And I didn't feel like I deserved it.''

He pulled his thoughts back from his mother and focused on the old man again. ''You didn't.''

A tired sigh escaped his father's lips. ''You're right. I didn't. Why do you think I drank?''

''I suppose you're going to blame that on Mom or society. Anyone but you.''

He shook his head. ''There you're wrong. It was me. All me. I drank because I knew I'd let your mother down. And you. I was afraid I wasn't enough of a man, enough of a father. And as a result, I did exactly what I was afraid of doing.''

Tightness assaulted Dex's throat. Alyson's words beat at the back of his mind. *You have to believe you deserve happiness. You have to believe happiness is more than just a dream.*

''Prison wasn't the price I had to pay for your mother's death. Living with what I've done, what I've lost through my own cowardice and stupidity, is the price. And it's a price I will never finish paying until I'm buried in the ground.''

Dex ran a hand over his face and leaned back in his chair. He'd gotten things wrong. He'd gotten things all wrong.

He'd been so careful to live a good, responsible life—a life different from his father's—and he hadn't escaped being like his father at all. The old man was right. In the matters that really counted he fit the old man's mold to a tee.

The disappointment, the bitterness, the judgment weren't reality, they were a nightmare. And Alyson wasn't a dream. *She* was reality. Her love. Her acceptance. The life she offered him. They were as real as the scarred wooden table in front of him. As real as his mother's love for him. And he'd been too stupid—too cowardly—to see it.

He looked into his father's eyes, blue like his own. "I never thought I'd thank you for anything. But I'm thanking you now."

His father's eyes crinkled around the corners and his mouth stretched into a tooth-baring grin. "For what?"

"For holding up that mirror and making me look."

ALYSON WATCHED Patrick's little chest rise and fall in perfect rhythm in the muted light coming from the closed curtains. The morning had been challenging, to say the least. Whether the baby was struggling to adjust to returning to his home and old routine or whether he was responding to the tension he could feel in his mommy was hard to say. But thankfully he was quiet for now. For now he was at peace.

Which was much more than she could say for herself.

She stepped into the hall and closed the door behind her. Shutting her eyes, she pressed her fingers to her lids until color mushroomed behind them. Pain pulsed in her head like the throbbing red and blue of police lights. But that was nothing compared to the pain pulsing with each beat of her heart.

Maybe it would have been better if she had never spent the past few days with Dex. Getting to know him again. To miss him. To love him. Maybe it would have been better if they'd never made it to the brink of a new life together only to discover that nothing had changed. Maybe a host of scenarios would have made things better. But she didn't think so.

Opening her eyes, she tiptoed down the hall and descended the stairs. She loved Dex. She had for years. And even if she hadn't been with him the past days, sharing with him, loving him, that love would still be there. And she would feel just as alone. Just as powerless.

She padded across the foyer's wood floor in stockinged feet and made her way into the living room. The day was still brilliant, warm rays filtering through the sheers covering the windows like a happy glow. As if the very weather was mocking her.

She crossed the living room to the window overlooking the street and pulled aside the sheers with one hand. Two police officers sat in one of the cars parked on the street and one officer sat on a park bench on the other side of the house. She should feel safe. Secure.

Then why did she feel so vulnerable? So powerless?

She let the curtain fall across the window. She knew the answer. And she couldn't do anything to solve the problem. Dex needed to sort through his own feelings, his own past. She couldn't do anything to smooth his path. Or to influence him. Or to make things turn out in the end.

And that's what scared her.

She crossed the room and lowered herself onto the couch. The cushions plumped around her, so soft, so comforting. She leaned her head back and closed her eyes. If only comforting her mind was so easy. If only comforting her heart....

A sound so soft she wasn't sure she'd heard it broke through her thoughts. The sound of a footstep.

In a house where she was supposed to be alone.

Her heart stilled in her chest. Opening her eyes,

she bolted off the couch and spun in the direction of the sound.

Andrew Clarke Smythe's hard blue eyes met her own. His fingers clutched a rag and on his belt draped a length of rope. "Hello, bitch. I've been waiting for this a long time. Now you're going to pay."

Fear clogged her throat. Shock paralyzed her limbs. She had to get away. She had to run. If she could reach the front door, the police outside would help her, save her.

Smythe moved into the room, blocking her path to the front door. "You know, I wasn't going to hurt the kid. I'm no sicko. If you wouldn't have screwed things up for me, I would have just left him for Nanny to raise. But you wouldn't let me do that, would you? Well, now you're all going to pay." He raised the rag and smiled. Chloroform.

She glanced at the front window. Thanks to the sheers, she couldn't see outside. And the police couldn't see what was happening inside, either. But if she could reach the window, if she could rip the sheers aside and get the officers' attention—

She dodged to the side and dashed in the direction of the front window.

Smythe reacted just as quickly. His footsteps thundered across the plush carpet behind her. His curse echoed in her ears.

She lunged forward, reaching for the curtain. Her

fingers brushed the fabric just as a fist closed around her hair.

He yanked, pulling her backward. Away from the window. Away from help. Pain ripped her scalp. Fingers bit into her throat. And the sickly sweet rag pressed over her face.

Chapter Seventeen

Alyson held her breath and forced her muscles to go limp. Every cell in her body clamored to fight. Every instinct told her to scream. But she couldn't fight and she couldn't scream. That would only make Smythe close his hands around her throat as he had before. Choke her until all she could do was gasp for breath. Gasp for oxygen. But she wouldn't get oxygen. She'd breathe in chloroform.

She had to stay awake. She had to find a way to save Patrick. To save herself. She couldn't let him hurt her baby.

Smythe finally pulled the cloth from her mouth and tossed it on the floor. He released her, letting her fall to the carpet in a heap, like a piece of discarded trash.

Her head hit the floor hard, the soft carpet cushioning just enough to keep her from plunging into blackness. She struggled to breathe without gasping for air.

"You think you're so much better than me, don't you, redhead bitch?" Smythe's smooth voice took on a guttural edge. "Well, we'll just see what you think when I'm finished with you. And we'll see what Harrington thinks when he finds you and the kid dead."

She bit the inside of her cheek to stop the scream building in her throat. Blood filled her mouth, its copper sweetness choking her. She had to bide her time. She had to catch Smythe off guard. It was her only chance.

He grasped the rope from his belt and tied a knot around one of her ankles. He pulled the knot tight, the rope biting into her leg. He wrenched her leg up tight behind her.

She remembered the dark lines around Connie Rasula's wrists and ankles. Oh, God, he planned to hog-tie her. Once he did that, she would be helpless. She could do nothing but watch as he did anything he wanted to her.

Watch and wait to die.

She had to make her move. She had to find an opening, or it would be too late. She tensed her muscles, waiting for her chance.

Smythe grabbed one of her wrists and twisted it behind her back.

Pain knifed through her shoulder. She stifled a cry of pain. Dizziness swam through her head. No. She couldn't give in to the pain. She couldn't let herself pass out. She had to concentrate. She forced herself to focus on Smythe's legs, his balance.

He shifted positions, stepping over her to get a better angle to tie the knot around her wrist. A knife blade flashed in his hand, poised to cut a section of rope.

Terror stabbed her. She couldn't think about the knife. She couldn't let herself imagine that steel blade slicing into her flesh. Into Patrick's flesh. She had to make her move. It was her only chance. Taking a deep breath, she grabbed his ankle with her free hand and lifted with all her strength.

Caught by surprise, Smythe toppled backward. He landed hard on the floor, the thump reverberating through the house. A curse erupted from his lips.

Alyson scrambled to her feet. Smythe was between her and the window. She spun in the other direction and raced for the door, dragging the rope behind her. She had to get outside. She had to alert police. It was her only chance. To save Patrick. To save Dex. And to save herself.

Her stockinged feet skidded on the hardwood floor. She could feel Smythe climb to his feet, she could hear him thundering behind her. Growing closer. Reaching for her.

He was going to be too late.

She lunged for the door. Her fingers closed around the brass knob.

The rope yanked tight and cut into her ankle. Her

foot skidded out from under her. She slammed into the closed door before crashing to the floor.

A LOUD CRASH echoed through the house, audible even above the whir of the lowering garage door. Dex's heart stilled for a moment and then erupted in a frenzy of beats.

There could be dozens of explanations for the sound. Alyson could have dropped a pot in the kitchen or knocked over a chair—anything. But Dex didn't think so.

Something was wrong.

He scrambled from the car and raced for the door to the kitchen. His lungs seized in his chest. Smythe couldn't be in the house. It was impossible. The police were still out front. He couldn't have gotten through their surveillance. Could he?

Dex burst into the kitchen. The house was still. Quiet. Leaving the door open behind him, he stole across the hardwood floor, trying to make his footsteps as silent as possible. If Smythe was in the house, he didn't want him to know he was back. The rapist wasn't very big, but he was strong, his body built to sinewy hardness in the prison weight room. Dex needed to get the jump on him.

Damn. If only he had his gun. If only he hadn't left it upstairs, safely locked away. If only he hadn't been so sure Alyson would be safe. So sure the police would protect her.

How the hell did Smythe get in the house?

A muffled gasp came from the direction of the living room.

Alyson.

Dex's gut clenched. If the bastard had hurt her, he didn't stand a chance. Dex would dismember him with his bare hands.

He turned the corner into the foyer. Circling the staircase, he reached the entrance to the living room.

Alyson lay on the floor. Smythe hunched over her, a rope in his hands. His full weight drove down on the knee he had planted in the center of her back.

Rage roared in Dex's ears and flashed red in the corners of his vision. He glanced at the front door. The police were still outside. The safest thing for him to do was to throw open the door and call them in. They had the guns and the manpower to neutralize Smythe.

He glanced back into the living room and took a step toward the door. Just then Smythe completed his knot and reached for something on his belt. Filtered sunlight glinted off a sharp, steel blade.

Dex froze. He had to take on Smythe himself. He couldn't summon the police. If he did, Smythe would use the knife on Alyson. He'd kill her right in front of Dex's eyes, long before the police burst through the door. Smythe would never allow himself to be captured or killed before he had his revenge.

Dex sucked in a sharp breath. He balled his hands into fists and tensed his muscles.

Dex sprang. Racing across the living room floor, he hurled himself at Smythe. He caught the rapist in the back with all his weight. Smythe careened to the floor, Dex on top of him.

Pain sliced into his thigh.

The knife.

The blade flashed in Smythe's hand, muted with blood. Ignoring the pain in his leg, Dex grabbed for Smythe's knife hand. His fingers closed around his muscular wrist. Grasping. Holding. Pinning his arm to the floor.

Smythe uttered a curse. He twisted and thrust backward.

Dex's free arm skidded on the soft carpet and then crumpled.

Smythe pushed backward again, rolling Dex onto his back. He came down hard, his back to Dex's chest, knocking the air from his lungs.

Gasping, Dex tried to focus. He had to hold Smythe's knife arm. He couldn't release his grip. If he did, he'd be dead.

Smythe twisted around to face Dex, struggling to wrench the knife free. He stabbed into the carpet, the blade nicking Dex's forearm.

Dex grunted. Blood oozed down his arm.

The knife flashed again. Smythe slashing and missing.

Dex's grip on Smythe's knife arm slipped. He couldn't hold on much longer. Gritting his teeth, he pounded his fist into Smythe's face. Once. Twice. Three times. Blood from Smythe's nose covered his knuckles, sticky and slick at the same time. But the rapist continued to struggle.

A hand reached over Smythe's forehead and covered his face. Fingers dug into his eyes.

Alyson.

She yanked Smythe's head back. With her other hand, she pressed a cloth over his face. Chloroform. Alyson was using his own chloroform rag against him.

Smythe thrashed, trying to escape the fumes, trying to break away.

Dex held on with all his strength. Just a minute or two and Smythe would be unconscious.

Time seemed to move in slow motion. Smythe's thrashing slowed. Finally it stopped. His body went limp and draped across Dex, pinning him to the carpet.

Dex looked up into Alyson's wide green eyes, so frightened yet so strong. Her fingers still dug into Smythe's eyes. Her hand still clamped the rag over his mouth and nose, knuckles white with exertion. "Is he out? Is it over?"

Dex nodded. "It's over. Thank God, it's over."

She exhaled a heavy breath and let the rag slip from her hand and fall to the floor. She pulled her fingers from Smythe's eyes. His head lolled forward onto Dex's chest. Alyson sat on the floor, staring at the blood on her fingertips as if she wasn't sure how it got there.

Dex pushed Smythe's body off and crawled to his knees. Blood oozed from his knife wounds, but he didn't care.

He moved to Alyson's side. Reaching her, he smoothed strands of auburn hair from her cheeks and slipped his arm around her, pulling her close.

Her gaze moved to the blood smeared over his skin, shirt and jeans. Fear flared in her eyes. "You're hurt." She struggled to climb to her feet, but he held her in place.

"I'm fine."

"No, you're not. You're cut and bleeding."

He almost smiled. It was so like Alyson to care about his welfare above everything else. She would give anything for him. Why hadn't he seen it before? And why hadn't he been willing to do the same for her? "The cuts aren't that deep. I'll be fine. We'll tend to them, but not now."

She searched his eyes, not understanding.

"Now we need to talk."

"Whatever it is, it can wait. You—"

He held a finger to her lips, halting the flow of words. "This has waited too long already. It can't wait any longer." He'd almost lost her. Almost lost the only thing he couldn't survive losing. And he wasn't going to waste another moment. Not before he told her how he felt. Not before he claimed her as his own. "I love you, Alyson."

She looked away from him, eyeing Smythe's prone body. "I love you, too, Dex. Are you sure he won't wake up?"

He laughed and glanced at the scum lying in a heap on the floor. He'd been so wrapped up in what he had to say to Alyson, in making her understand, that he'd pushed Smythe from his mind. "After what you did to him, I'm sure. But if you like, we can walk out to the porch and summon the police while we talk."

She nodded. Arm tight around his waist, she stepped toward the door.

He limped by her side. This arrangement wasn't his idea of romantic, but it didn't matter. He needed to tell her how he felt, to get on with the rest of their lives. And he wouldn't wait. Not one more minute. "Like I said before, I love you, Alyson."

She looked up at him, her hair falling back from her face. Her eyes were still wide, tears of relief pooling in the corners. She'd been through so much. The hell Dex had put her through the last two years, the kidnapping of her baby, and now Smythe's attack. And by pure willpower, she'd survived it all.

His throat closed. How could he possibly tell her

all he felt? "I know you're not a dream, that what we have together isn't a dream."

A slight smile lifted the corners of her mouth.

"You were right this morning when you said I never felt I deserved happiness. I didn't. I was too busy assigning blame to my father, to myself. It never occurred to me that reality could be different from the way I saw it. It never occurred to me that in a way, I was making my own misery."

Alyson's hand found his arm, her fingers stroking his skin as if encouraging him to go on.

"When you came into my life, you didn't fit with the misery I'd planned for myself. So I was always waiting for proof that I was right, that what you and I had was a mistake."

"And you found it."

"Yes. And if I hadn't, I would have made something up. Anything to keep seeing the world the way I told myself it was."

"And now?"

"Now I see the world doesn't have to be that way. You showed me that, Alyson."

Her eyes searched his. Concern creased her brow and compressed her lips.

"I saw my father today." He still hadn't worked out all of his feelings about his father. Hell, that would probably take years. But at least he had a start.

"And?"

"He reminded me of one very important person I've forgotten in all this. My mother." He stopped walking. Trailing his fingers over Alyson's skin, he cupped her smooth cheek. "She was very much like you. Loving. Giving. Ready to see the best in people, no matter if they deserved it or not."

"I wish I could have met her."

"You would have loved her. And she would have loved you."

Alyson's lips softened into a smile.

"I've had good things in my life. And I can reach out and accept good into my life again." He gripped the doorknob.

She nodded, tears pooling in her eyes and transforming them into a shimmering green. "I know you can."

His heart seized in his chest. She believed in him. She always had. He'd just been too blind to see it. He gathered her hand in his. "I always thought that if this time ever came, I'd get down on one knee with flowers and music and a diamond ring to give you."

A tear broke loose and trickled down her cheek. "Music and flowers and jewelry are overrated sometimes."

"I'm glad you feel that way, because I can't wait another minute." He swallowed into a dry throat.

"Will you marry me, Alyson? Will you and Patrick be the good in my life? Will you be my family?"

She wiped her cheek with the back of one hand and gave him a watery smile. "On one condition."

"Anything."

"That you be the good in my life, as well."

He pulled open the door. "Just try to stop me."

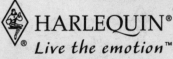

Two women in jeopardy...
Two shattering secrets...
Two dramatic stories...

VEILS OF DECEIT

USA TODAY bestselling author

JASMINE CRESSWELL

B.J. DANIELS

A riveting volume of scandalous secrets, political intrigue and
unforgettable passion that you will not want to miss!

Look for VEILS OF DECEIT in April 2003
at your favorite retail outlet.

HARLEQUIN®
Makes any time special®

Visit us at www.eHarlequin.com

PHVOD

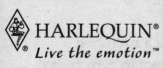

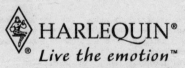